Mugby Junction

D0817132

Mugby Junction

Charles Dickens

with
Andrew Halliday
Charles Collins
Hesba Stretton
Amelia Edwards

ET REMOTISSIMA PROPE

Hesperus Classics

Hesperus Classics

Published by Hesperus Press Limited

4 Rickett Street, London SW6 1RU

www.hesperuspress.com

First published in *All the Year Round* in 1866

First published by Hesperus Press Limited, 2005

Foreword © Robert Macfarlane, 2005

Designed by Fraser Muggeridge studio

Typeset by William Chamberlain

Printed in Jordan by the Jordan National Press

ISBN: 1-84391-129-9

CONTENTS

On a hot June day in 1865, eighteen months before he began writing *Mugby Junction*, Dickens was involved in what would become known as the Staplehurst Disaster. Accompanied by his mistress, Ellen Ternan, and her mother, Dickens was travelling by train on the Folkestone to London line. That day, maintenance work was being carried out on the line where it crossed a viaduct over the River Beult. The foreman in charge of the repairs had consulted the wrong timetable, and he was not expecting Dickens' train for another two hours. Rails had been prised from the viaduct rail-bed, leaving a forty-two-foot gap.

Unwarned, Dickens' train hit the gap in the track at a speed of around twenty-five miles per hour. Six of the seven first-class carriages were pitched into the river. Only the coach carrying Dickens was saved. Held by its coupling to the second-class carriage behind it, it came to rest at an angle, tilted on the brink of the gap.

Once he and the Ternans had managed to escape their precarious carriage, Dickens clambered down to the river, and began to help the injured, of whom there were many. He filled his top hat with water and a flask with brandy, and for three hours he moved between the casualties, doing what he could to comfort them. At one point he gave a lady with a bloodied face, who was resting under a tree, a sip of brandy. The next time he passed her she was dead. When Dickens bent to help a man with a fractured skull lying on the grass, the man murmured 'I am gone' and died.

The after-effects of the Staplehurst crash on Dickens were serious. 'My father's nerves,' his daughter Maisie remarked after his death, 'never really were the same again.' For weeks following the accident, he suffered nervous shakes and sudden sweats. He became prey to panic attacks while travelling in any sort of vehicle. Though he continued to take trains, he often chose slow trains rather than expresses. When he did make rail journeys, he would frequently get off several stations before his actual destination and walk the remaining miles.

A shadow of this last neurosis can be seen in the masterfully strange opening scene of *Mugby Junction*. At three o'clock 'of a tempestuous morning', a nameless traveller descends for an unknown reason onto a darkened platform at Mugby Junction. This traveller – who we will come to know as Jackson – reveals that he has arrived at Mugby by chance. In flight from an old life of rigour and discipline, he boarded a train in London with the intention of alighting at a randomly chosen station. 'The traveller,' Dickens writes of Jackson, 'had been, like many others, carried [there] on the steam winds and the iron tides.'

These new powers of dispersal – for good and for ill – possessed by the railways form the binding theme of the eight stories in *Mugby Junction*. The first of the stories was published in the Christmas 1866 number of *All the Year Round* (a magazine edited by Dickens) and sold an astonishing 250,000 copies in its initial week. Dickens wrote three more of the stories; the other four – which are, it must be said, of undulating quality – were by Andrew Halliday, Charles Collins, Hesba Stretton and Amelia Edwards, regular contributors to *All the Year Round*.

Mugby Junction itself is a make-believe Midlands railway station. Seven lines, we learn, run into Mugby, and seven run out of it, and these charmed numbers are our first clue that Mugby is a place which hovers halfway between the fairy tale and the real. For all the lovingly precise description of its platforms, tunnels, refreshment rooms and signal boxes, we realise Mugby is an existential crossroads as well as a material one – 'a Junction,' as Dickens remarks, 'of many branches, invisible as well as visible, and joined… to an endless number of byways.'

After his small-hours arrival at Mugby, Jackson decides to stay in the area for a few days. When he meets and falls into a chaste but intense relationship with a young invalid named Phoebe, those days turn into weeks, and he begins to investigate the area and its inhabitants. Like a journalist beating the streets for scoops, or an early psychogeographer on the *dérive*, Jackson wanders around Mugby, asking its inhabitants – the post-office worker, the signalman, the engineer, the engine-driver – for their accounts of how they came to be there, and where they hope to go. These testimonies comprise the remaining episodes of the collection: its 'branch lines'. They are, as Dickens puts it, 'what was seen, heard, or otherwise picked up by the gentleman for Nowhere in his careful study of the Junction', and they mingle oral history, reportage, sensation fiction, anthropology and ghost story.

Given Dickens' experiences at Staplehurst, it is surprising how many of these stories present the railways as a force for good – an innovation able to join and to heal. Bed-bound Phoebe, for instance, relishes the imaginative connection which 'the Great Junction' provides with the wider world. 'I don't see it under the foot of the hill,' she tells Jackson, 'but I can very often hear it, and I always know it is there. It seems to join me, in a way, to I don't know how many places and things that *I* shall never see.' Jackson, too, is changed for the better by the railways. When he first reaches Mugby, he is crabby and pinched – a classic Dickensian character in need of temperamental reform. After a week in the Junction, however, he has been invigorated; where before he 'had walked blindly brooding', he 'now had eyes and thoughts for a new external world'.

Another indicator of the railways' great power to alter human life is that, in *Mugby Junction*, people are – metaphorically speaking – continually turning into trains, and trains into people. So there is a man called 'Lamps', while the Junction itself has 'gas eyes'. Jackson is first introduced to us as a man who has a 'brooding carriage', but who has decided to change 'his station in life', and in the final story, a maddened engineer on a runaway train feels as if his 'blood was on fire, as if every nerve was iron': as he pounds along the rails, he is becoming his machine.

Dickens has fun, too, making his prose resemble trains – shunting words around, coupling clauses together, and setting sentences into motion, before bringing them to a halt on the buffers of a full stop – as in this fine passage from the opening scene:

'A place replete with shadowy shapes, this Mugby Junction in the black hours of the four-and-twenty. Mysterious goods trains, covered with palls and gliding on like vast weird funerals, conveying themselves guiltily away from the presence of the few lighted lamps, as if their freight had come to a secret and unlawful end. Half-miles of coal pursuing in a Detective manner, following when they lead, stopping when they stop, backing when they back. Red-hot embers showering out upon the ground, down this dark avenue, and down the other, as if torturing fires were being raked clear; concurrently, shrieks and groans and grinds invading the ear, as if the tortured were at the height of their suffering.'

For all its optimism and good cheer, however, *Mugby Junction* is also grimly alert to the powers of the railways to tear people apart, as well as to connect them. The slightly overheated closing story, 'The Engineer', describes how two best friends from a tiny rural village start working on the railways, and end up living in Genoa, both infatuated with the same femme fatale. Love-blinded, one murders the other, and spends the rest of his life in penance. 'Altogether, since 1841, I've killed seven men and boys,' begins the engine-driver's testimony, strikingly. 'It ain't many in all those years.' The gentle and affecting story of the signalman ends with his death, when he is 'cut down' from behind by a train as it emerges from a tunnel.

The different 'storylines' of *Mugby Junction* differently register what one character calls the 'perilous and marvellous' qualities of the railways. Together, they form a collection which celebrates the potential of the new technology to link previously distant people and places, but which is also anxious at the new types of violence it has brought into being.

– Robert Macfarlane, 2005

Mugby Junction

BARBOX BROTHERS
[by Charles Dickens]

1

'Guard! What place is this?'

'Mugby Junction, sir.'

'A windy place!'

'Yes, it mostly is, sir.'

'And looks comfortless indeed!'

'Yes, it generally does, sir.'

'Is it a rainy night still?'

'Pours, sir.'

'Open the door. I'll get out.'

'You'll have, sir,' said the guard, glistening with drops of wet, and looking at the tearful face of his watch by the light of his lantern as the traveller descended, 'three minutes here.'

'More, I think – for I am not going on.'

'Thought you had a through ticket, sir?'

'So I have, but I shall sacrifice the rest of it. I want my luggage.'

'Please to come to the van and point it out, sir. Be good enough to look very sharp, sir. Not a moment to spare.'

The guard hurried to the luggage van, and the traveller hurried after him. The guard got into it, and the traveller looked into it.

'Those two large black portmanteaus in the corner where your light shines. Those are mine.'

'Name upon 'em, sir?'

'Barbox Brothers.'

'Stand clear, sir, if you please. One. Two. Right!'

Lamp waved. Signal lights ahead already changing. Shriek from engine. Train gone.

'Mugby Junction!' said the traveller, pulling up the woollen muffler round his throat with both hands. 'At past three o'clock of a tempestuous morning! So!'

He spoke to himself. There was no one else to speak to. Perhaps, though, had there been anyone else to speak to, he would have preferred to speak to himself. Speaking to himself he spoke to a man within five years of fifty either way, who had turned grey too soon, like a neglected fire; a man of pondering habit, brooding carriage of the head, and suppressed internal voice; a man with many indications on him of having been much alone.

He stood unnoticed on the dreary platform, except by the rain and by the wind. Those two vigilant assailants made a rush at him. 'Very well,' said he, yielding. 'It signifies nothing to me to what quarter I turn my face.'

Thus, at Mugby Junction, at past three o'clock of a tempestuous morning, the traveller went where the weather drove him.

Not but what he could make a stand when he was so minded, for, coming to the end of the roofed shelter (it is of considerable extent at Mugby Junction), and looking out upon the dark night, with a yet darker spirit-wing of storm beating its wild way through it, he faced about and held his own as ruggedly in the difficult direction as he had held it in the easier one. Thus, with a steady step, the traveller went up and down, up and down, up and down, seeking nothing, and finding it.

A place replete with shadowy shapes, this Mugby Junction in the black hours of the four-and-twenty. Mysterious goods trains, covered with palls and gliding on like vast weird funerals, conveying themselves guiltily away from the presence of the few lighted lamps, as if their freight had come to a secret and unlawful end. Half-miles of coal pursuing in a detective manner, following when they lead, stopping when they stop, backing when they back. Red-hot embers showering out upon the ground, down this dark avenue, and down the other, as if torturing fires were being raked clear; concurrently, shrieks and groans and grinds invading the ear, as if the tortured were at the height of their suffering. Iron-barred cages full of cattle jangling by midway, the drooping beasts with horns entangled, eyes frozen with terror, and mouths too: at least they have long icicles (or what seem so) hanging from their lips. Unknown languages in the air, conspiring in red, green and white characters. An earthquake, accompanied with thunder and lightning, going up express to London. Now, all quiet, all rusty, wind and rain in possession, lamps extinguished, Mugby Junction dead and indistinct, with its robe drawn over its head, like Caesar.

Now, too, as the belated traveller plodded up and down, a shadowy train went by him in the gloom – which was no other than the train of a life. From whatsoever intangible deep cutting or dark tunnel it emerged, here it came, unsummoned and unannounced, stealing upon him, and passing away into obscurity. Here, mournfully went by a child who had never had a childhood or known a parent, inseparable from a youth with a bitter sense of his namelessness, coupled to a man the enforced business of whose best years had been distasteful and oppressive, linked to an ungrateful friend, dragging after him a woman once beloved. Attendant, with many a clank and wrench, were lumbering cares, dark meditations, huge dim disappointments, monotonous years, a long jarring line of the discords of a solitary and unhappy existence.

'... Yours, sir?'

The traveller recalled his eyes from the waste into which they had been staring, and fell back a step or so under the abruptness, and perhaps the chance appropriateness, of the question.

'Oh! My thoughts were not here for the moment. Yes. Yes. Those two portmanteaus are mine. Are you a porter?'

'On porter's wages, sir. But I am Lamps.'

The traveller looked a little confused.

'Who did you say you are?'

'Lamps, sir,' showing an oily cloth in his hand, as further explanation.

'Surely, surely. Is there any hotel or tavern here?'

'Not exactly here, sir. There *is* a refreshment room here, but –' Lamps, with a mighty serious look, gave his head a warning roll that plainly added, 'but it's a blessed circumstance for you that it's not open.'

'You couldn't recommend it, I see, if it was available?'

'Ask your pardon, sir. If it was?...'

'Open?'

'It ain't my place, as a paid servant of the company, to give my opinion on any of the company's toepics' – he pronounced it more like toothpicks – 'beyond lamp-ile and cottons,' returned Lamps in a confidential tone; 'but speaking as a man, I wouldn't recommend my father (if he was to come to life again) to go and try how he'd be treated at the Refreshment Room. Not speaking as a man, no, I would *not*.'

The traveller nodded conviction. 'I suppose I can put up in the town? There is a town here?' For the traveller (though a stay-at-home compared with most travellers) had been, like many others, carried on the steam winds and the iron tides through that Junction before, without having ever, as one might say, gone ashore there.

'Oh yes, there's a town, sir. Anyways, there's town enough to put up in. But,' following the glance of the other at his luggage, 'this is a very dead time of the night with us, sir. The deadest time. I might a'most call it our deadest and buriedest time.'

'No porters about?'

'Well, sir, you see,' returned Lamps, confidential again, 'they in general goes off with the gas. That's how it is. And they seem to have overlooked you, through your walking to the furder end of the platform. But in about twelve minutes or so she may be up.'

'Who may be up?'

'The three forty-two, sir. She goes off in a sidin' till the Up X passes, and then she' – here an air of hopeful vagueness pervaded Lamps – 'doos all as lays in her power.'

'I doubt if I comprehend the arrangement.'

'I doubt if anybody do, sir. She's a parliamentary, sir. And, you see, a parliamentary, or a skirmishun –'

'Do you mean an excursion?'

'That's it, sir. – A parliamentary or a skirmishun, she mostly *doos* go off into a sidin'. But, when she *can* get a chance, she's whistled out of it, and she's whistled up into doin' all as' – Lamps again wore the air of a highly sanguine man who hoped for the best – 'all as lays in her power.'

He then explained that porters on duty, being required to be in attendance on the parliamentary matron in question, would doubtless turn up with the gas. In the meantime, if the gentleman would not very much object to the smell of lamp oil, and would accept the warmth of his little room – the gentleman, being by this time very cold, instantly closed with the proposal.

A greasy little cabin it was, suggestive, to the sense of smell, of a cabin in a whaler. But there was a bright fire burning in its rusty grate, and on the floor there stood a wooden stand of newly trimmed and lighted lamps, ready for carriage service. They made a bright show, and their light, and the warmth, accounted for the popularity of the room, as borne witness to by many impressions of velveteen trousers on a form by the fire, and many rounded smears and smudges of stooping velveteen shoulders on the adjacent wall. Various untidy shelves accommodated a quantity of lamps and oil cans, and also a fragrant collection of what looked like the pocket handkerchiefs of the whole lamp family.

As Barbox Brothers (so to call the traveller on the warranty of his luggage) took his seat upon the form, and warmed his now ungloved hands at the fire, he glanced aside at a little deal desk, much blotched with ink, which his elbow touched. Upon it were some scraps of coarse paper, and a superannuated steel pen in very reduced and gritty circumstances.

From glancing at the scraps of paper, he turned involuntarily to his host, and said, with some roughness:

'Why, you are never a poet, man!'

Lamps had certainly not the conventional appearance of one, as he stood modestly rubbing his squab nose with a handkerchief so exceedingly oily that he might have been in the act of mistaking himself for one of his charges. He was a spare man of about the Barbox Brothers time of life, with his features whimsically drawn upward as if they were attracted by the roots of his hair. He had a peculiarly shining transparent complexion, probably occasioned by constant oleaginous application; and his attractive hair, being cut short, and being grizzled, and standing straight up on end as if it in its turn were attracted by some invisible magnet above it, the top of his head was not very unlike a lamp wick.

'But to be sure, it's no business of mine,' said Barbox Brothers. 'That was an impertinent observation on my part. Be what you like.'

'Some people, sir,' remarked Lamps in a tone of apology, 'are sometimes what they don't like.'

'Nobody knows that better than I do,' sighed the other. 'I have been what I don't like all my life.'

'When I first took, sir,' resumed Lamps, 'to composing little comic songs like –'

7

Barbox Brothers eyed him with great disfavour.

'…To composing little comic songs like – and what was more hard – to singing 'em afterwards,' said Lamps, 'it went against the grain at that time, it did indeed.'

Something that was not all oil here shining in Lamps's eye, Barbox Brothers withdrew his own a little disconcerted, looked at the fire, and put a foot on the top bar. 'Why did you do it, then?' he asked, after a short pause – abruptly enough, but in a softer tone. 'If you didn't want to do it, why did you do it? Where did you sing them? Public house?'

To which Mr Lamps returned the curious reply: 'Bedside.'

At this moment, while the traveller looked at him for elucidation, Mugby Junction started suddenly, trembled violently, and opened its gas eyes. 'She's got up!' Lamps announced, excited. 'What lays in her power is sometimes more and sometimes less; but it's laid in her power to get up tonight, by George!'

The legend 'Barbox Brothers', in large white letters on two black surfaces, was very soon afterwards trundling on a truck through a silent street and, when the owner of the legend had shivered on the pavement half an hour – what time the porter's knocks at the inn door knocked up the whole town first, and the inn last – he groped his way into the close air of a shut-up house, and so groped between the sheets of a shut-up bed that seemed to have been expressly refrigerated for him when last made.

2

'You remember me, Young Jackson?'

'What do I remember if not you? You are my first remembrance. It was you who told me that was my name. It was you who told me that on every twentieth of December my life had a penitential anniversary in it called a birthday. I suppose the last communication was truer than the first!'

'What am I like, Young Jackson?'

'You are like a blight all through the year, to me. You hard-lined, thin-lipped, repressive, changeless woman with a wax mask on. You are like the Devil to me – most of all when you teach me religious things, for you make me abhor them.'

'You remember me, Mr Young Jackson?' In another voice from another quarter.

'Most gratefully, sir. You were the ray of hope and prospering ambition in my life. When I attended your course, I believed that I should come to be a great healer, and I felt almost happy – even though I was still the one boarder in the house with that horrible mask, and ate and drank in silence and constraint with the mask before me, every day. As I had done every, every, every day, through my school time and from my earliest recollection.'

'What am I like, Mr Young Jackson?'

'You are like a superior being to me. You are like nature beginning to reveal herself to me. I hear you again, as one of the hushed crowd of young men kindling under the power of your presence and knowledge, and you bring into my eyes the only exultant tears that ever stood in them.'

'You remember me, Mr Young Jackson?' In a grating voice from quite another quarter.

'Too well. You made your ghostly appearance in my life one day, and announced that its course was to be suddenly and wholly changed. You showed me which was my wearisome seat in the galley of Barbox Brothers. (When *they* were, if they ever were, is unknown to me; there was nothing of them but the name when I bent to the oar.) You told me what I was to do, and what to be paid; you told me afterwards, at intervals of years, when I was to sign for the firm, when I became a partner, when I became the firm. I know no more of it, or of myself.'

'What am I like, Mr Young Jackson?'

'You are like my father, I sometimes think. You are hard enough and cold enough so to have brought up an acknowledged son. I see your scanty figure, your close brown suit, and your tight brown wig; but you, too, wear a wax mask to your death. You never by a chance remove it – it never by a chance falls off – and I know no more of you.'

Throughout this dialogue, the traveller spoke to himself at his window in the morning, as he had spoken to himself at the Junction overnight. And as he had then looked in the darkness – a man who had turned grey too soon, like a neglected fire – so he now looked in the sunlight, an ashier grey, like a fire which the brightness of the sun put out.

The firm of Barbox Brothers had been some offshoot or irregular branch of the public notary and bill-broking tree. It had gained for itself a griping reputation before the days of Young Jackson, and the reputation had stuck to it and to him. As he had imperceptibly come into possession of the dim den up in the corner of a court off Lombard Street, on whose grimy windows the inscription Barbox Brothers had for many long years daily interposed itself between him and the sky, so he had insensibly found himself a personage held in chronic distrust, whom it was essential to screw tight to every transaction in which he engaged, whose word was never to be taken without his attested bond, whom all dealers with openly set up guards and wards against. This character had come upon him through no act of his own. It was as if the original Barbox had stretched himself down upon the office floor, and had thither caused to be conveyed Young Jackson in his sleep, and had there effected a metempsychosis and exchange of persons with him. The discovery – aided in its turn by the deceit of the only woman he had ever loved, and the deceit of the only friend he had ever made, who eloped from him to be married together – the discovery, so followed up, completed what his earliest rearing had begun. He shrank, abashed, within the form of Barbox, and lifted up his head and heart no more.

But he did at last effect one great release in his condition. He broke the oar he had plied so long, and he scuttled and sank the galley. He prevented the gradual retirement of an old conventional business from him by taking the initiative and retiring from it. With enough to live on (though, after all, with not too much), he obliterated the firm of Barbox Brothers from the pages of the Post Office Directory and the face of the earth, leaving nothing of it but its name on two portmanteaus.

'For one must have some name in going about, for people to pick up,' he explained to Mugby High Street, through the inn window, 'and that name at least was real once. Whereas Young Jackson! – Not to mention its being a sadly satirical misnomer for Old Jackson.'

He took up his hat and walked out, just in time to see, passing along on the opposite side of the way, a velveteen man, carrying his day's dinner in a small bundle that might have been larger without suspicion of gluttony, and pelting away towards the Junction at a great pace.

'There's Lamps!' said Barbox Brothers. 'And by the by…'

Ridiculous, surely, that a man so serious, so self-contained, and not yet three days emancipated from a routine of drudgery, should stand rubbing his chin in the street, in a brown study about comic songs.

'Bedside?' said Barbox Brothers testily. 'Sings them at the bedside? Why at the bedside, unless he goes to bed drunk? Does, I shouldn't wonder. But it's no business of mine. Let me see. Mugby Junction, Mugby Junction. Where shall I go next? As it came into my head last night when I woke from an uneasy sleep in the carriage and found myself here, I can go anywhere from here. Where shall I go? I'll go and look at the Junction by daylight. There's no hurry, and I may like the look of one line better than another.'

But there were so many lines. Gazing down upon them from a bridge at the Junction, it was as if the concentrating companies formed a great industrial exhibition of the works of extraordinary ground spiders that spun iron. And then so many of the lines went such wonderful ways, so crossing and curving among one another, that the eye lost them. And then some of them appeared to start with the fixed intention of going five hundred miles, and all of a sudden gave it up at an insignificant barrier, or turned off into a workshop. And then others, like intoxicated men, went a little way very straight, and surprisingly slewed round and came back again. And then others were so chock-full of trucks of coal, others were so blocked with trucks of casks, others were so gorged with trucks of ballast, others were so set apart for wheeled objects like immense iron cotton-reels; while others were so bright and clear, and others were so delivered over to rust and ashes and idle wheel-barrows out of work, with their legs in the air (looking much like their masters on strike), that there was no beginning, middle or end to the bewilderment.

Barbox Brothers stood puzzled on the bridge, passing his right hand across the lines on his forehead, which multiplied while he looked down, as if the railway lines were getting themselves photographed on that sensitive plate. Then was heard a distant ringing of bells and blowing of whistles. Then, puppet-looking heads of men popped out of boxes in perspective, and popped in again. Then, prodigious wooden razors, set up on end, began shaving the atmosphere. Then, several loco-motive engines in several directions began to scream and be agitated.

Then, along one avenue a train came in. Then, along another two trains appeared that didn't come in, but stopped without. Then, bits of trains broke off. Then, a struggling horse became involved with them. Then, the locomotives shared the bits of trains, and ran away with the whole.

'I have not made my next move much clearer by this. No hurry. No need to make up my mind today, or tomorrow, nor yet the day after. I'll take a walk.'

It fell out somehow (perhaps he meant it should) that the walk tended to the platform at which he had alighted, and to Lamps's room. But Lamps was not in his room. A pair of velveteen shoulders were adapting themselves to one of the impressions on the wall by Lamps's fireplace, but otherwise the room was void. In passing back to get out of the station again, he learnt the cause of this vacancy, by catching sight of Lamps on the opposite line of railway, skipping along the top of a train, from carriage to carriage, and catching lighted namesakes thrown up to him by a coadjutor.

'He is busy. He has not much time for composing or singing comic songs this morning, I take it.'

The direction he pursued now was into the country, keeping very near to the side of one great line of railway, and within easy view of others. 'I have half a mind,' he said, glancing around, 'to settle the question from this point, by saying, "I'll take this set of rails, or that, or t'other, and stick to it." They separate themselves from the confusion, out here, and go their ways.'

Ascending a gentle hill of some extent, he came to a few cottages. There, looking about him as a very reserved man might who had never looked about him in his life before, he saw some six or eight young children come merrily trooping and whooping from one of the cottages and disperse. But not until they had all turned at the little garden gate and kissed their hands to a face at the upper window – a low window enough, although the upper – for the cottage had but a storey of one room above the ground.

Now, that the children should do this was nothing; but that they should do this to a face lying on the sill of the open window, turned towards them in a horizontal position, and apparently only a face, was something noticeable. He looked up at the window again. Could only see a very fragile, though a very bright face, lying on one cheek on the window sill. The delicate smiling face of a girl or woman. Framed in long bright brown hair, round which was tied a light blue band or fillet, passing under the chin.

He walked on, turned back, passed the window again, shyly glanced up again. No change. He struck off by a winding branch-road at the top of the hill – which he must otherwise have descended – kept the cottages in view, worked his way round at a distance so as to come out once more into the main road and be obliged to pass the cottages again. The face still lay on the window sill, but not so much inclined towards him. And now there were a pair of delicate hands too. They had the action of performing on some musical instrument, and yet it produced no sound that reached his ears.

'Mugby Junction must be the maddest place in England,' said Barbox Brothers, pursuing his way down the hill. 'The first thing I find here is a railway porter who composes comic songs to sing at his bedside. The second thing I find here is a face, and a pair of hands playing a musical instrument that *don't* play!'

The day was a fine bright day in the early beginning of November, the air was clear and inspiriting, and the landscape was rich in beautiful colours. The prevailing colours in the court off Lombard Street, London City, had been few and sombre. Sometimes, when the weather elsewhere was very bright indeed, the dwellers in those tents enjoyed a pepper-and-salt-coloured day or two, but their atmosphere's usual wear was slate or snuff colour.

He relished his walk so well that he repeated it next day. He was a little earlier at the cottage than on the day before, and he could hear the children upstairs singing to a regular measure and clapping out the time with their hands.

'Still, there is no sound of any musical instrument,' he said, listening at the corner, 'and yet I saw the performing hands again as I came by. What are the children singing? Why, good Lord, they can never be singing the multiplication table?'

They were though, and with infinite enjoyment. The mysterious face had a voice attached to it, which occasionally led or set the children right. Its musical cheerfulness was delightful. The measure at length stopped, and was succeeded by a murmuring of young voices, and then by a short song which he made out to be about the current month of the year, and about what work it yielded to the labourers in the fields and farmyards. Then there was a stir of little feet, and the children came trooping and whooping out, as on the previous day. And again, as on the previous day, they all turned at the garden gate, and kissed their hands – evidently to the face on the window sill, though Barbox Brothers from his retired post of disadvantage at the corner could not see it.

But, as the children dispersed, he cut off one small straggler – a brown-faced boy with flaxen hair – and said to him:

'Come here, little one. Tell me, whose house is that?'

The child, with one swarthy arm held up across his eyes, half in shyness and half ready for defence, said from behind the inside of his elbow:

'Phoebe's.'

'And who,' said Barbox Brothers, quite as much embarrassed by his part in the dialogue as the child could possibly be by his, 'is Phoebe?'

To which the child made answer: 'Why, Phoebe, of course.'

The small but sharp observer had eyed his questioner closely, and had taken his moral measure. He lowered his guard, and rather assumed a tone with him, as having discovered him to be an unaccustomed person in the art of polite conversation.

'Phoebe,' said the child, 'can't be anybobby else but Phoebe. Can she?'

'No, I suppose not.'

'Well,' returned the child, 'then why did you ask me?'

Deeming it prudent to shift his ground, Barbox Brothers took up a new position.

'What do you do there? Up there in that room where the open window is. What do you do there?'

'Cool,' said the child.

'Eh?'

'Co-o-ol,' the child repeated in a louder voice, lengthening out the word with a fixed look and great emphasis, as much as to say: 'What's the use of your having grown up, if you're such a donkey as not to understand me?'

'Ah! School, school,' said Barbox Brothers. 'Yes, yes, yes. And Phoebe teaches you?'

The child nodded.

'Good boy.'

'Tound it out, have you?' said the child.

'Yes, I have found it out. What would you do with twopence, if I gave it you?'

'Pend it.'

The knock-down promptitude of this reply leaving him not a leg to stand upon, Barbox Brothers produced the twopence with great lameness, and withdrew in a state of humiliation.

But, seeing the face on the window sill as he passed the cottage, he acknowledged its presence there with a gesture, which was not a nod, not a bow, not a removal of his hat from his head, but was a diffident compromise between or struggle with all three. The eyes in the face seemed amused, or cheered, or both, and the lips modestly said: 'Good day to you, sir.'

'I find I must stick for a time to Mugby Junction,' said Barbox Brothers with much gravity, after once more stopping on his return road to look at the lines where they went their several ways so quietly. 'I can't make up my mind yet which iron road to take. In fact, I must get a little accustomed to the Junction before I can decide.'

So, he announced at the inn that he was 'going to stay on, for the present', and improved his acquaintance with the Junction that night, and again next morning, and again next night and morning – going down to the station, mingling with the people there, looking about him down all the avenues of railway, and beginning to take an interest in the incomings and outgoings of the trains. At first, he often put his head into Lamps's little room, but he never found Lamps there. A pair or two of velveteen shoulders he usually found there, stooping over the fire, sometimes in connection with a clasped knife and a piece of bread and meat; but the answer to his enquiry, 'Where's Lamps?' was either that he was 't'other side the line' or that it was his off-time, or (in the latter case) his own personal introduction to another Lamps who was not his

Lamps. However, he was not so desperately set upon seeing Lamps now, but he bore the disappointment. Nor did he so wholly devote himself to his severe application to the study of Mugby Junction as to neglect exercise. On the contrary, he took a walk every day, and always the same walk. But the weather turned cold and wet again, and the window was never open.

3

At length, after a lapse of some days, there came another streak of fine bright hardy autumn weather. It was a Saturday. The window was open, and the children were gone. Not surprising, this, for he had patiently watched and waited at the corner until they *were* gone.

'Good day,' he said to the face; absolutely getting his hat clear off his head this time.

'Good day to you, sir.'

'I am glad you have a fine sky again to look at.'

'Thank you, sir. It is kind of you.'

'You are an invalid, I fear?'

'No, sir. I have very good health.'

'But are you not always lying down?'

'Oh yes, I am always lying down, because I cannot sit up. But I am not an invalid.'

The laughing eyes seemed highly to enjoy his great mistake.

'Would you mind taking the trouble to come in, sir? There is a beautiful view from this window. And you would see that I am not at all ill – being so good as to care.'

It was said to help him, as he stood irresolute, but evidently desiring to enter, with his diffident hand on the latch of the garden gate. It did help him, and he went in.

The room upstairs was a very clean white room with a low roof. Its only inmate lay on a couch that brought her face to a level with the window. The couch was white too; and her simple dress or wrapper being light blue, like the band around her hair, she had an ethereal look, and a fanciful appearance of lying among clouds. He felt that she instinctively perceived him to be by habit a downcast taciturn man; it was another help to him to have established that understanding so easily, and got it over.

There was an awkward constraint upon him, nevertheless, as he touched her hand, and took a chair at the side of her couch.

'I see now,' he began, not at all fluently, 'how you occupy your hands. Only seeing you from the path outside, I thought you were playing upon something.'

She was engaged in very nimbly and dexterously making lace. A lace pillow lay upon her breast – and the quick movements and changes of her hands upon it, as she worked, had given them the action he had misinterpreted.

'That is curious,' she answered, with a bright smile, 'for I often fancy, myself, that I play tunes while I am at work.'

'Have you any musical knowledge?'

She shook her head.

'I think I could pick out tunes, if I had any instrument, which could be made as handy to me as my lace pillow. But I dare say I deceive myself. At all events, I shall never know.'

'You have a musical voice. Excuse me – I have heard you sing.'

'With the children?' she answered, slightly colouring. 'Oh yes. I sing with the dear children, if it can be called singing.'

Barbox Brothers glanced at the two small forms in the room, and hazarded the speculation that she was fond of children, and that she was learned in new systems of teaching them. 'Very fond of them,' she said, shaking her head again; 'but I know nothing of teaching beyond the interest I have in it and the pleasure it gives me when they learn. Perhaps your overhearing my little scholars sing some of their lessons has led you so far astray as to think me a grand teacher? Ah! I thought so! No, I have only read and been told about that system. It seemed so pretty and pleasant – and to treat them so like the merry robins they are – that I took up with it in my little way. You don't need to be told what a very little way mine is, sir,' she added with a glance at the small forms and round the room.

All this time her hands were busy at her lace pillow. As they still continued so, and as there was a kind of substitute for conversation in the click and play of its pegs, Barbox Brothers took the opportunity of observing her. He guessed her to be thirty. The charm of her transparent face and large bright brown eyes was, not that they were passively resigned, but that they were actively and thoroughly cheerful. Even her busy hands, which of their own thinness alone might have besought compassion, plied their task with a gay courage that made mere compassion an unjustifiable assumption of superiority, and an impertinence.

He saw her eyes in the act of rising towards his, and he directed his towards the prospect, saying: 'Beautiful indeed!'

'Most beautiful, sir. I have sometimes had a fancy that I would like to sit up, for once, only to try how it looks to an erect head. But what a foolish fancy that would be to encourage! It cannot look more lovely to anyone than it does to me.'

Her eyes were turned to it as she spoke, with most delighted admiration and enjoyment. There was not a trace in it of any sense of deprivation.

'And those threads of railway, with their puffs of smoke and steam changing places so fast, make it so lively for me,' she went on. 'I think of the number of people who *can* go where they wish, on their business or their pleasure; I remember that the puffs make signs to me that they are actually going while I look; and that enlivens the prospect with abundance of company, if I want company. There is the great Junction, too. I don't see it under the foot of the hill, but I can very often hear it, and I always know it is there. It seems to join me, in a way, to I don't know how many places and things that *I* shall never see.'

With an abashed kind of idea that it might have already joined himself to something he had never seen, he said constrainedly: 'Just so.'

'And so you see, sir,' pursued Phoebe, 'I am not the invalid you thought me, and I am very well off indeed.'

'You have a happy disposition,' said Barbox Brothers, perhaps with a slight excusatory touch for his own disposition.

'Ah! But you should know my father,' she replied. 'His is the happy disposition! – Don't mind, sir!' For his reserve took the alarm at a step upon the stairs, and he distrusted that he would be set down for a troublesome intruder. 'This is my father coming.'

The door opened, and the father paused there.

'Why, Lamps!' exclaimed Barbox Brothers, starting from his chair. 'How do you do, Lamps?'

To which Lamps responded: 'The gentleman for Nowhere! How do you *do*, sir?'

And they shook hands, to the greatest admiration and surprise of Lamps's daughter.

'I have looked you up half a dozen times since that night,' said Barbox Brothers, 'but have never found you.'

'So I've heerd on, sir, so I've heerd on,' returned Lamps. 'It's your being noticed so often down at the Junction, without taking any train, that has begun to get you the name among us of the gentleman for Nowhere. No offence in my having called you by it when took by surprise, I hope, sir?'

'None at all. It's as good a name for me as any other you could call me by. But may I ask you a question in the corner here?'

Lamps suffered himself to be led aside from his daughter's couch by one of the buttons of his velveteen jacket.

'Is this the bedside where you sing your songs?'

Lamps nodded.

The gentleman for Nowhere clapped him on the shoulder, and they faced about again.

'Upon my word, my dear,' said Lamps then to his daughter, looking from her to her visitor, 'it is such an amaze to me, to find you brought acquainted with this gentleman, that I must (if this gentleman will excuse me) take a rounder.'

Mr Lamps demonstrated in action what this meant, by pulling out his oily handkerchief rolled up in the form of a ball, and giving himself an elaborate smear, from behind the right ear, up the cheek, across the forehead, and down the other cheek to behind his left ear. After this operation, he shone exceedingly.

'It's according to my custom when particular warmed up by any agitation, sir,' he offered by way of apology. 'And really, I am throwed into that state of amaze by finding you brought acquainted with Phoebe, that I – that I think I will, if you'll excuse me, take another rounder.' Which he did, seeming to be greatly restored by it.

They were now both standing by the side of her couch, and she was working at her lace pillow. 'Your daughter tells me,' said Barbox Brothers, still in a half-reluctant shamefaced way, 'that she never sits up.'

'No, sir, nor never has done. You see, her mother (who died when she was a year and two months old) was subject to very bad fits, and as she had never mentioned to me that she *was* subject to fits, they couldn't be guarded against. Consequently, she dropped the baby when took, and this happened.'

'It was very wrong of her,' said Barbox Brothers with a knitted brow, 'to marry you, making a secret of her infirmity.'

'Well, sir,' pleaded Lamps, in behalf of the long-deceased. 'You see, Phoebe and me, we have talked that over too. And Lord bless us! Such a number on us has our infirmities, what with fits, and what with misfits, of one sort and another, that if we confessed to 'em all before we got married, most of us might never get married.'

'Might not that be for the better?'

'Not in this case, sir,' said Phoebe, giving her hand to her father.

'No, not in this case, sir,' said her father, patting it between his own.

'You correct me,' returned Barbox Brothers with a blush; 'and I must look so like a brute that at all events it would be superfluous in me to confess to *that* infirmity. I wish you would tell me a little more about yourselves. I hardly knew how to ask it of you, for I am conscious that I have a bad stiff manner, a dull discouraging way with me, but I wish you would.'

'With all our hearts, sir,' returned Lamps, gaily, for both. 'And first of all, that you may know my name –'

'Stay!' interposed the visitor with a slight flush. 'What signifies your name? Lamps is name enough for me. I like it. It is bright and expressive. What do I want more?'

'Why to be sure, sir,' returned Lamps. 'I have in general no other name down at the Junction; but I thought, on account of your being here as a first-class single, in a private character, that you might –'

The visitor waved the thought away with his hand, and Lamps acknowledged the mark of confidence by taking another rounder.

'You are hard-worked, I take for granted?' said Barbox Brothers, when the subject of the rounder came out of it much dirtier than he went into it.

Lamps was beginning, 'Not particular so –' when his daughter took him up.

'Oh yes, sir, he is very hard-worked. Fourteen, fifteen, eighteen hours a day. Sometimes twenty-four hours at a time.'

'And you,' said Barbox Brothers, 'what with your school, Phoebe, and what with your lace-making –'

'But my school is a pleasure to me,' she interrupted, opening her brown eyes wider, as if surprised to find him so obtuse. 'I began it when I was but a child, because it brought me and other children into company, don't you see? *That* was not work. I carry it on still, because it keeps children about me. *That* is not work. I do it as love, not as work. Then my lace pillow' – her busy hands had stopped, as if her argument required all her cheerful earnestness, but now went on again at the name – 'it goes with my thoughts when I think, and it goes with my tunes when I hum any, and *that's* not work. Why, you yourself thought it was music, you know, sir. And so it is to me.'

'Everything is!' cried Lamps, radiantly. 'Everything is music to her, sir.'

'My father is, at any rate,' said Phoebe, exultingly pointing her thin forefinger at him. 'There is more music in my father than there is in a brass band.'

'I say! My dear! It's very fillyillially done, you know; but you are flattering your father,' he protested, sparkling.

'No I am not, sir, I assure you. No I am not. If you could hear my father sing, you would know I am not. But you never will hear him sing, because he never sings to anyone but me. However tired he is, he always sings to me when he comes home. When I lay here long ago, quite a poor little broken doll, he used to sing to me. More than that, he used to make songs, bringing in whatever little jokes we had between us. More than that, he often does so to this day. Oh! I'll tell of you, father, as the gentleman has asked about you. He is a poet, sir.'

'I shouldn't wish the gentleman, my dear,' observed Lamps, for the moment turning grave, 'to carry away that opinion of your father, because it might look as if I was given to asking the stars in a molloncolly manner what they was up to. Which I wouldn't at once waste the time, and take the liberty, my dear.'

'My father,' resumed Phoebe, amending her text, 'is always on the bright side, and the good side. You told me, just now, I had a happy disposition. How can I help it?'

'Well – but, my dear,' returned Lamps argumentatively, 'how can *I* help it? Put it to yourself, sir. Look at her. Always as you see her now. Always working – and after all, sir, for but a very few shillings a week – always contented, always lively, always interested in others, of all sorts. I said, this moment, she was always as you see her now. So she is, with a difference that comes to much the same. For when it's my Sunday off and the morning bells have done ringing, I hear the prayers and thanks read in the touchingest way, and I have the hymns sung to me – so soft, sir, that you couldn't hear 'em out of this room – in notes that seem to me, I am sure, to come from heaven and go back to it.'

It might have been merely through the association of these words with their sacredly quiet time, or it might have been through the larger association of the words with the Redeemer's presence beside the bedridden; but here her dexterous fingers came to a stop on the lace pillow, and clasped themselves around his neck as he bent down. There was great natural sensibility in both father and daughter, the visitor could easily see; but each made it, for the other's sake, retiring, not demonstrative; and perfect cheerfulness, intuitive or acquired, was either the first or second nature of both. In a very few moments, Lamps was taking another rounder with his comical features beaming, while Phoebe's laughing eyes (just a glistening speck or so upon their lashes) were again directed by turns to him, and to her work, and to Barbox Brothers.

'When my father, sir,' she said brightly, 'tells you about my being interested in other people, even though they know nothing about me – which, by the by, I told you myself – you ought to know how that comes about. That's my father's doing.'

'No, it isn't!' he protested.

'Don't you believe him, sir – yes, it is. He tells me of everything he sees down at his work. You would be surprised what a quantity he gets together for me every day. He looks into the carriages, and tells me how the ladies are dressed – so that I know all the fashions! He looks into the carriages, and tells me what pairs of lovers he sees, and what new-married couples on their wedding trip – so that I know all about that! He collects chance newspapers and books – so that I have plenty to read! He tells me about the sick people who are travelling to try to get better – so that I know all about them! In short, as I began by saying, he tells me everything he sees and makes out, down at his work, and you can't think what a quantity he does see and make out.'

'As to collecting newspapers and books, my dear,' said Lamps, 'it's clear I can have no merit in that, because they're not my perquisites. You see, sir, it's this way: a guard, he'll say to me, "Hallo, here you are, Lamps. I've saved this paper for your daughter. How is she a-going on?" A head porter, he'll say to me, "Here! Catch hold, Lamps. Here's a couple of wollumes for your daughter. Is she pretty much where she were?" And that's what makes it double welcome, you see. If she had a thousand pound in a box, they wouldn't trouble themselves about her; but being what she is – that is, you understand,' Lamps added, somewhat hurriedly, 'not having a thousand pound in a box – they take thought for her. And as concerning the young pairs, married and unmarried, it's only natural I should bring home what little I can about *them*, seeing that there's not a couple of either sort in the neighbourhood that don't come of their own accord to confide in Phoebe.'

She raised her eyes triumphantly to Barbox Brothers as she said:

'Indeed, sir, that is true. If I could have got up and gone to church, I don't know how often I should have been a bridesmaid. But if I could have done that, some girls in love might have been jealous of me – and, as it is, no girl is jealous of me. And my pillow would not have been half as ready to put the piece of cake under, as I always find it,' she added, turning her face on it with a light sigh, and a smile at her father.

The arrival of a little girl, the biggest of the scholars, now led to an understanding on the part of Barbox Brothers that she was the domestic of the cottage and had come to take active measures in it, attended by a pail that might have extinguished her, and a broom three times her height. He therefore rose to take his leave, and took it, saying that if Phoebe had no objection, he would come again.

He had muttered that he would come 'in the course of his walks'. The course of his walks must have been highly favourable to his return, for he returned after an interval of a single day.

'You thought you would never see me any more, I suppose?' he said to Phoebe as he touched her hand, and sat down by her couch.

'Why should I think so?' was her surprised rejoinder.

'I took it for granted you would mistrust me.'

'For granted, sir? Have you been so much mistrusted?'

'I think I am justified in answering yes. But I may have mistrusted, too, on my part. No matter just now. We were speaking of the Junction last time. I have passed hours there since the day before yesterday.'

'Are you now the gentleman for Somewhere?' she asked with a smile.

'Certainly for Somewhere – but I don't yet know Where. You would never guess what I am travelling from. Shall I tell you? I am travelling from my birthday.'

Her hands stopped in her work, and she looked at him with incredulous astonishment.

'Yes,' said Barbox Brothers, not quite easy in his chair, 'from my birthday. I am, to myself, an unintelligible book with the earlier chapters all torn out, and thrown away. My childhood had no grace of childhood, my youth had no charm of youth, and what can be expected from such a lost beginning?' His eyes meeting hers as they were addressed intently to him, something seemed to stir within his breast, whispering: 'Was this bed a place for the graces of childhood and the charms of youth to take to kindly? Oh, shame, shame!'

'It is a disease with me,' said Barbox Brothers, checking himself, and making as though he had a difficulty in swallowing something, 'to go wrong about that. I don't know how I came to speak of that. I hope it is because of an old misplaced confidence in one of your sex involving an old bitter treachery. I don't know. I am all wrong together.'

Her hands quietly and slowly resumed their work. Glancing at her, he saw that her eyes were thoughtfully following them.

'I am travelling from my birthday,' he resumed, 'because it has always been a dreary day to me. My first free birthday coming round some five or six weeks hence, I am travelling to put its predecessors far behind me, and to try to crush the day – or, at all events, put it out of my sight, by heaping new objects on it.'

As he paused, she looked at him; but only shook her head as being quite at a loss.

'This is unintelligible to your happy disposition,' he pursued, abiding by his former phrase as if there were some lingering virtue of self-defence in it. 'I knew it would be, and am glad it is. However, on this travel of mine (in which I mean to pass the rest of my days, having abandoned all thought of a fixed home), I stopped, as you heard from your father, at the Junction here. The extent of its ramifications quite confused me as to whither I should go *from* here. I have not yet settled, being still perplexed among so many roads. What do you think I mean to do? How many of the branching roads can you see from your window?'

Looking out, full of interest, she answered, 'Seven.'

'Seven,' said Barbox Brothers, watching her with a grave smile. 'Well! I propose to myself, at once to reduce the gross number to those very seven, and gradually to fine them down to one – the most promising for me – and to take that.'

'But how will you know, sir, which *is* the most promising?' she asked, with her brightened eyes roving over the view.

'Ah!' said Barbox Brothers with another grave smile, and considerably improving in his ease of speech. 'To be sure. In this way. Where your father can pick up so much every day for a good purpose, I may once and again pick up a little for an indifferent purpose. The gentleman for Nowhere must become still better known at the Junction. He shall continue to explore it, until he attaches something that he has seen, heard or found out at the head of each of the seven roads to the road itself. And so his choice of a road shall be determined by his choice among his discoveries.'

Her hands still busy, she again glanced at the prospect, as if it comprehended something that had not been in it before, and laughed as if it yielded her new pleasure.

'But I must not forget,' said Barbox Brothers, 'having got so far, to ask a favour. I want your help in this expedient of mine. I want to bring you what I pick up at the heads of the seven roads that you lie here looking npare notes with you about it. May I? They say two

/ than one. I should say myself that probably depends

is concerned. But I am quite sure, though we are so newly

, that your head and your father's have found out better

oebe, than ever mine of itself discovered.'

She gave him her sympathetic right hand, in perfect rapture with his proposal, and eagerly and gratefully thanked him.

'That's well!' said Barbox Brothers. 'Again I must not forget, having got so far, to ask a favour. Will you shut your eyes?'

Laughing playfully at the strange nature of the request, she did so.

'Keep them shut,' said Barbox Brothers, going softly to the door, and coming back. 'You are on your honour, mind, not to open your eyes until I tell you that you may?'

'Yes! On my honour.'

'Good. May I take your lace pillow from you for a minute?'

Still laughing and wondering, she removed her hands from it, and he put it aside.

'Tell me. Did you see the puffs of smoke and steam made by the morning fast train yesterday on road number seven from here?'

'Behind the elm trees and the spire?'

'That's the road,' said Barbox Brothers, directing his eyes towards it.

'Yes. I watched them melt away.'

'Anything unusual in what they expressed?'

'No!' she answered merrily.

'Not complimentary to me, for I was in that train. I went – don't open your eyes – to fetch you this, from the great ingenious town. It is not half so large as your lace pillow, and lies easily and lightly in its place. These little keys are like the keys of a miniature piano, and you supply the air required with your left hand. May you pick out delightful music from it, my dear! For the present – you can open your eyes now – goodbye!'

In his embarrassed way, he closed the door upon himself, and only saw, in doing so, that she ecstatically took the present to her bosom and caressed it. The glimpse gladdened his heart, and yet saddened it; for so might she, if her youth had flourished in its natural course, have taken to her breast that day the slumbering music of her own child's voice.

BARBOX BROTHERS AND CO.
[by Charles Dickens]

With goodwill and earnest purpose, the gentleman for Nowhere began, on the very next day, his researches at the heads of the seven roads. The results of his researches, as he and Phoebe afterwards set them down in fair writing, hold their due places in this veracious chronicle. But they occupied a much longer time in the getting together than they ever will in the perusal. And this is probably the case with most reading matter, except when it is of that highly beneficial kind (for posterity) which is 'thrown off in a few moments of leisure' by the superior poetic geniuses who scorn to take prose pains.

It must be admitted, however, that Barbox by no means hurried himself. His heart being in his work of good nature, he revelled in it. There was the joy, too (it was a true joy to him), of sometimes sitting by, listening to Phoebe as she picked out more and more discourse from her musical instrument, and as her natural taste and ear refined daily upon her first discoveries. Besides being a pleasure, this was an occupation, and in the course of weeks it consumed hours. It resulted that his dreaded birthday was close upon him before he had troubled himself any more about it.

The matter was made more pressing by the unforeseen circumstance that the councils held (at which Mr Lamps, beaming most brilliantly, on a few rare occasions assisted) respecting the road to be selected were, after all, in no wise assisted by his investigations. For he had connected this interest with this road, or that interest with the other, but could deduce no reason from it for giving any road the preference. Consequently, when the last council was held, that part of the business stood, in the end, exactly where it had stood in the beginning.

'But, sir,' remarked Phoebe, 'we have only six roads after all. Is the seventh road dumb?'

'The seventh road? Oh!' said Barbox Brothers, rubbing his chin. 'That is the road I took, you know, when I went to get your little present. That is *its* story, Phoebe.'

'Would you mind taking that road again, sir?' she asked with hesitation.

'Not in the least; it is a great high road after all.'

'I should like you to take it,' returned Phoebe with a persuasive smile, 'for the love of that little present which must ever be so dear to me. I should like you to take it, because that road can never be again like any other road to me. I should like you to take it in remembrance of your having done me so much good, of your having made me so much happier! If you leave me by the road you travelled when you went to do me this great kindness,' sounding a faint chord as she spoke, 'I shall feel, lying here watching at my window, as if it must conduct you to a prosperous end, and bring you back some day.'

'It shall be done, my dear; it shall be done.'

So at last the gentleman for Nowhere took a ticket for Somewhere, and his destination was the great ingenious town.

He had loitered so long about the Junction that it was the eighteenth of December when he left it. 'High time,' he reflected, as he seated himself in the train, 'that I started in earnest! Only one clear day remains between me and the day I am running away from. I'll push onward for the hill country tomorrow. I'll go to Wales.'

It was with some pains that he placed before himself the undeniable advantages to be gained in the way of novel occupation for his senses from misty mountains, swollen streams, rain, cold, a wild seashore, and rugged roads. And yet he scarcely made them out as distinctly as he could have wished. Whether the poor girl, in spite of her new resource, her music, would have any feeling of loneliness upon her now – just at first – that she had not had before; whether she saw those very puffs of steam and smoke that he saw, as he sat in the train thinking of her; whether her face would have any pensive shadow on it as they died out of the distant view from her window; whether, in telling him he had done her so much good, she had not unconsciously corrected his old moody bemoaning of his station in life by setting him thinking that a man might be a great healer, if he would, and yet not be a great doctor – these and other similar meditations got between him and his Welsh picture. There was within him, too, that dull sense of vacuity which follows separation from an object of interest and cessation of a pleasant pursuit – and this sense, being quite new to him, made him restless. Further, in losing Mugby Junction, he had found himself again; and he was not the more enamoured of himself for having lately passed his time in better company.

But surely here, not far ahead, must be the great ingenious town. This crashing and clashing that the train was undergoing, and this coupling onto it of a multitude of new echoes, could mean nothing less than approach to the great station. It did mean nothing less. After some stormy flashes of town lightning, in the way of swift revelations of red brick blocks of houses, high red brick chimney shafts, vistas of red brick railway arches, tongues of fire, blots of smoke, valleys of canal and hills of coal, there came the thundering in at the journey's end.

Having seen his portmanteaus safely housed in the hotel he chose, and having appointed his dinner hour, Barbox Brothers went out for a walk in the busy streets. And now it began to be suspected by him that Mugby Junction was a Junction of many branches, invisible as well as visible, and had joined him to an endless number of byways. For whereas he would, but a little while ago, have walked these streets blindly brooding, he now had eyes and thoughts for a new external world. How the many toiling people lived, and loved, and died; how wonderful it was to consider the various trainings of eye and hand, the nice distinctions of sight and touch, that separated them into classes of workers, and even into classes of workers at subdivisions of one complete whole which combined their many intelligences and forces, though of itself but some cheap object of use or ornament in common life; how good it was to know that such assembling in a multitude on their part and such contribution of their several dexterities towards a civilising end did not deteriorate them as it was the fashion of the supercilious mayflies of humanity to pretend, but engendered among them a self-respect and yet a modest desire to be much wiser than they were (the first evinced in their well-balanced bearing and manner of speech when he stopped to ask a question; the second, in the announcements of their popular studies and amusements on the public walls) – these considerations, and a host of such, made his walk a memorable one. 'I too am but a little part of a great whole,' he began to think; 'and to be serviceable to myself and others, or to be happy, I must cast my interest into, and draw it out of, the common stock.'

Although he had arrived at his journey's end for the day by noon, he had since insensibly walked about the town so far and so long that the lamplighters were now at their work in the streets, and the shops were sparkling up brilliantly. Thus reminded to turn towards his quarters, he was in the act of doing so, when a very little hand crept into his, and a very little voice said:

'Oh! If you please, I am lost!'

He looked down, and saw a very little fair-haired girl.

'Yes,' she said, confirming her words with a serious nod. 'I am indeed. I am lost!'

Greatly perplexed, he stopped, looked about him for help, descried none and said, bending low: 'Where do you live, my child?'

'I don't know where I live,' she returned. 'I am lost.'

'What is your name?'

'Polly.'

'What is your other name?'

The reply was prompt, but unintelligible.

Imitating the sound as he caught it, he hazarded the guess, 'Trivits?'

'Oh no!' said the child, shaking her head. 'Nothing like that.'

'Say it again, little one.'

An unpromising business. For this time it had quite a different sound. He made the venture, ' Paddens?'

'Oh no!' said the child. 'Nothing like that.'

'Once more. Let us try it again, dear.'

A most hopeless business. This time it swelled into four syllables. 'It can't be Tappitarver?' said Barbox Brothers, rubbing his head with his hat in discomfiture.

'No! It ain't,' the child quietly assented.

On her trying this unfortunate name once more, with extraordinary efforts at distinctness, it swelled into eight syllables at least.

'Ah! I think,' said Barbox Brothers with a desperate air of resignation, 'that we had better give it up.'

'But I am lost,' said the child, nestling her little hand more closely in his, 'and you'll take care of me, won't you?'

If ever a man were disconcerted by division between compassion on the one hand, and the very imbecility of irresolution on the other, here the man was. 'Lost!' he repeated, looking down at the child. 'I am sure *I* am. What is to be done?'

'Where do *you* live?' asked the child, looking up at him wistfully.

'Over there,' he answered, pointing vaguely in the direction of his hotel.

'Hadn't we better go there?' said the child.

'Really,' he replied, 'I don't know but what we had.'

So they set off, hand in hand. He, through comparison of himself against his little companion, with a clumsy feeling on him as if he had just developed into a foolish giant. She, clearly elevated in her own tiny opinion by having got him so neatly out of his embarrassment.

'We are going to have dinner when we get there, I suppose?' said Polly.

'Well,' he rejoined, 'I – yes, I suppose we are.'

'Do you like your dinner?' asked the child.

'Why, on the whole,' said Barbox Brothers, 'yes, I think I do.'

'I do mine,' said Polly. 'Have you any brothers and sisters?'

'No. Have you?'

'Mine are dead.'

'Oh!' said Barbox Brothers. With that absurd sense of unwieldiness of mind and body weighing him down, he would have not known how to pursue the conversation beyond this curt rejoinder, but that the child was always ready for him.

'What,' she asked, turning her soft hand coaxingly in his, 'are you going to do to amuse me after dinner?'

'Upon my soul, Polly,' exclaimed Barbox Brothers, very much at a loss, 'I have not the slightest idea!'

'Then I tell you what,' said Polly. 'Have you got any cards at your house?'

'Plenty,' said Barbox Brothers, in a boastful vein.

'Very well. Then I'll build houses, and you shall look at me. You mustn't blow, you know.'

'Oh no!' said Barbox Brothers. 'No, no, no. No blowing. Blowing's not fair.'

He flattered himself that he had said this pretty well for an idiotic monster; but the child, instantly perceiving the awkwardness of his attempt to adapt himself to her level, utterly destroyed his hopeful opinion of himself by saying compassionately: 'What a funny man you are!'

Feeling, after this melancholy failure, as if he every minute grew bigger and heavier in person, and weaker in mind, Barbox gave himself up for a bad job. No giant ever submitted more meekly to be led in triumph by all-conquering Jack than he to be bound in slavery to Polly.

'Do you know any stories?' she asked him.

He was reduced to the humiliating confession: 'No.'

'What a dunce you must be, mustn't you?' said Polly.

He was reduced to the humiliating confession: 'Yes.'

'Would you like me to teach you a story? But you must remember it, you know, and be able to tell it right to somebody else afterwards.'

He professed that it would afford him the highest mental gratification to be taught a story, and that he would humbly endeavour to retain it in his mind. Whereupon Polly, giving her hand a new little turn in his, expressive of settling down for enjoyment, commenced a long romance, of which every relishing clause began with the words: 'So this', or, 'And so this'. As, 'So this boy'; or, 'So this fairy'; or, 'And so this pie was four yards round, and two yards and a quarter deep'. The interest of the romance was derived from the intervention of this fairy to punish this boy for having a greedy appetite. To achieve which purpose, this fairy made this pie, and this boy ate and ate and ate, and his cheeks swelled and swelled and swelled. There were many tributary circumstances, but the forcible interest culminated in the total consumption of this pie, and the bursting of this boy. Truly he was a fine sight, Barbox Brothers, with serious attentive face, and ear bent down, much jostled on the pavements of the busy town, but afraid of losing a single incident of the epic, lest he should be examined in it by and by, and found deficient.

Thus they arrived at the hotel. And there he had to say at the bar, and said awkwardly enough, 'I have found a little girl!'

The whole establishment turned out to look at the little girl. Nobody knew her; nobody could make out her name, as she set it forth – except one chambermaid, who said it was Constantinople – which it wasn't.

'I will dine with my young friend in a private room,' said Barbox

Brothers to the hotel authorities, 'and perhaps you will be so good as to let the police know that the pretty baby is here. I suppose she is sure to be enquired for soon, if she has not been already. Come along, Polly.'

Perfectly at ease and peace, Polly came along, but, finding the stairs rather stiff work, was carried up by Barbox Brothers. The dinner was a most transcendent success, and the Barbox sheepishness, under Polly's directions how to mince her meat for her, and how to diffuse gravy over the plate with a liberal and equal hand, was another fine sight.

'And now,' said Polly, 'while we are at dinner, you be good, and tell me that story I taught you.'

With the tremors of a Civil Service examination upon him, and very uncertain indeed, not only as to the epoch at which the pie appeared in history, but also as to the measurements of that indispensable fact, Barbox Brothers made a shaky beginning, but under encouragement did very fairly. There was a want of breadth observable in his rendering of the cheeks, as well as the appetite, of the boy; and there was a certain tameness in his fairy, referable to an undercurrent of desire to account for her. Still, as the first lumbering performance of a good-humoured monster, it passed muster.

'I told you to be good,' said Polly, 'and you are good, ain't you?'

'I hope so,' replied Barbox Brothers.

Such was his deference that Polly, elevated on a platform of sofa cushions in a chair at his right hand, encouraged him with a pat or two on the face from the greasy bowl of her spoon, and even with a gracious kiss. In getting on her feet upon her chair, however, to give him this last reward, she toppled forward among the dishes, and caused him to exclaim as he effected her rescue: 'Gracious Angels! Whew! I thought we were in the fire, Polly!'

'What a coward you are, ain't you?' said Polly, when replaced.

'Yes, I am rather nervous,' he replied. 'Whew! Don't, Polly! Don't flourish your spoon, or you'll go over sideways. Don't tilt up your legs when you laugh, Polly, or you'll go over backwards. Whew! Polly, Polly, Polly,' said Barbox Brothers, nearly succumbing to despair, 'we are environed with dangers!'

Indeed, he could descry no security from the pitfalls that were yawning for Polly, but in proposing to her, after dinner, to sit upon a low stool. 'I will, if you will,' said Polly. So, as peace of mind should go before all, he begged the waiter to wheel aside the table, bring a pack of cards, a couple of footstools and a screen, and close in Polly and himself before the fire, as it were in a snug room within the room. Then, finest sight of all, was Barbox Brothers on his footstool, with a pint decanter on the rug, contemplating Polly as she built successfully, and growing blue in the face with holding his breath, lest he should blow the house down.

'How you stare, don't you?' said Polly in a houseless pause.

Detected in the ignoble fact, he felt obliged to admit, apologetically: 'I am afraid I was looking rather hard at you, Polly.'

'Why do you stare?' asked Polly.

'I cannot,' he murmured to himself, 'recall why – I don't know, Polly.'

'You must be a simpleton to do things and not know why, mustn't you?' said Polly.

In spite of which reproof, he looked at the child again intently, as she bent her head over her card structure, her rich curls shading her face. 'It is impossible,' he thought, 'that I can ever have seen this pretty baby before. Can I have dreamt of her? In some sorrowful dream?'

He could make nothing of it. So he went into the building trade as a journeyman under Polly, and they built three storeys high, four storeys high – even five.

'I say – who do you think is coming?' asked Polly, rubbing her eyes after tea.

He guessed: 'The waiter?'

'No,' said Polly, 'the dustman. I am getting sleepy.'

A new embarrassment for Barbox Brothers!

'I don't think I am going to be fetched tonight,' said Polly; 'what do you think?'

He thought not, either. After another quarter of an hour, the dustman not merely impending, but actually arriving, recourse was had to the Constantinopolitan chambermaid, who cheerily undertook that the child should sleep in a comfortable and wholesome room, which she herself would share.

'And I know you will be careful, won't you,' said Barbox Brothers, as a new fear dawned upon him, 'that she don't fall out of bed?'

Polly found this so highly entertaining that she was under the necessity of clutching him round the neck with both arms as he sat on his footstool picking up the cards and rocking him to and fro, with her dimpled chin on his shoulder.

'Oh what a coward you are, ain't you?' said Polly. 'Do *you* fall out of bed?'

'N-not generally, Polly.'

'No more do I.'

With that, Polly gave him a reassuring hug or two to keep him going, and then giving that confiding mite of a hand of hers to be swallowed up in the hand of the Constantinopolitan chambermaid, trotted off, chattering, without a vestige of anxiety.

He looked after her, had the screen removed and the table and chairs replaced, and still looked after her. He paced the room for half an hour. 'A most engaging little creature, but it's not that. A most winning little voice, but it's not that. That has much to do with it, but there is something more. How can it be that I seem to know this child? What was it she imperfectly recalled to me when I felt her touch in the street and, looking down at her, saw her looking up at me?'

'Mr Jackson!'

With a start he turned towards the sound of the subdued voice, and saw his answer standing at the door.

'Oh, Mr Jackson, do not be severe with me! Speak a word of encouragement to me, I beseech you.'

'You are Polly's mother.'

'Yes.'

Yes. Polly herself might come to this, one day. As you see what the rose was in its faded leaves – as you see what the summer growth of the woods was in their wintry branches – so Polly might be traced, one day, in a careworn woman like this, with her hair turned grey. Before him were the ashes of a dead fire that had once burnt bright. This was the woman he had loved. This was the woman he had lost. Such had been the constancy of his imagination to her, so had time spared her under its withholding, that now, seeing how roughly the inexorable hand had struck her, his soul was filled with pity and amazement.

He led her to a chair, and stood leaning on a corner of the chimney piece, with his head resting on his hand and his face half averted.

'Did you see me in the street and show me to your child?' he asked.

'Yes.'

'Is the little creature, then, a party to deceit?'

'I hope there is no deceit. I said to her, "We have lost our way, and I must try to find mine by myself. Go to that gentleman and tell him you are lost. You shall be fetched by and by." Perhaps you have not thought how very young she is?'

'She is very self-reliant.'

'Perhaps because she is so young.'

He asked, after a short pause, 'Why did you do this?'

'Oh, Mr Jackson, do you ask me? In the hope that you might see something in my innocent child to soften your heart towards me. Not only towards me, but towards my husband.'

He suddenly turned about, and walked to the opposite end of the room. He came back again with a slower step, and resumed his former attitude, saying: 'I thought you had emigrated to America?'

'We did. But life went ill with us there, and we came back.'

'Do you live in this town?'

'Yes. I am a daily teacher of music here. My husband is a book-keeper.'

'Are you – forgive my asking – poor?'

'We earn enough for our wants. That is not our distress. My husband is very, very ill of a lingering disorder. He will never recover –'

'You check yourself. If it is for want of the encouraging word you spoke of, take it from me. I cannot forget the old time, Beatrice.'

'God bless you!' she replied, with a burst of tears, and gave him her trembling hand.

'Compose yourself. I cannot be composed if you are not, for to see you weep distresses me beyond expression. Speak freely to me. Trust me.'

She shaded her face with her veil, and after a little while spoke calmly. Her voice had the ring of Polly's.

'It is not that my husband's mind is at all impaired by his bodily suffering, for I assure you that is not the case. But in his weakness, and in his knowledge that he is incurably ill, he cannot overcome the ascendancy of one idea. It preys upon him, embitters every moment of his painful life, and will shorten it.'

She stopping, he said again: 'Speak freely to me. Trust me.'

'We have had five children before this darling, and they all lie in their little graves. He believes that they have withered away under a curse, and that it will blight this child like the rest.'

'Under what curse?'

'Both I and he have it on our conscience that we tried you very heavily, and I do not know but that, if I were as ill as he, I might suffer in my mind as he does. This is the constant burden: "I believe, Beatrice, I was the only friend that Mr Jackson ever cared to make, though I was so much his junior. The more influence he acquired in the business, the higher he advanced me, and I was alone in his private confidence. I came between him and you, and I took you from him. We were both secret, and the blow fell when he was wholly unprepared. The anguish it caused a man so compressed must have been terrible; the wrath it awakened, inappeasable. So a curse came to be invoked on our poor, pretty little flowers, and they fall."'

'And you, Beatrice,' he asked, when she had ceased to speak, and there had been a silence afterwards, 'how say you?'

'Until within these few weeks I was afraid of you, and I believed that you would never, never forgive.'

'Until within these few weeks,' he repeated. 'Have you changed your opinion of me within these few weeks?'

'Yes.'

'For what reason?'

'I was getting some pieces of music in a shop in this town, when, to my terror, you came in. As I veiled my face and stood in the dark end of the shop, I heard you explain that you wanted a musical instrument for a bedridden girl. Your voice and manner were so softened, you showed such interest in its selection, you took it away yourself with so much tenderness of care and pleasure, that I knew you were a man with a most gentle heart. Oh, Mr Jackson, Mr Jackson, if you could have felt the refreshing rain of tears that followed for me!'

Was Phoebe playing at that moment on her distant couch? He seemed to hear her.

'I enquired in the shop where you lived, but could get no information. As I had heard you say that you were going back by the next train (but you did not say where), I resolved to visit the station at about that time of day, as often as I could, between my lessons, on the chance of seeing you again. I have been there very often, but saw you no more until today. You were meditating as you walked the street, but the calm expression of your face emboldened me to send my child to you. And when I saw you bend your head to speak tenderly to her, I prayed to God to forgive me for having ever brought a sorrow on it. I now pray to you to forgive me, and to forgive my husband. I was very young, he was young too, and in the ignorant hardihood of such a time of life we don't know what we do to those who have undergone more discipline. You generous man! You good man! So to raise me up and make nothing of my crime against you!' – for he would not see her on her knees, and soothed her as a kind father might have soothed an erring daughter – 'Thank you, bless you, thank you!'

When he next spoke, it was after having drawn aside the window curtain and looked out awhile. Then, he only said:

'Is Polly asleep?'

'Yes. As I came in, I met her going away upstairs, and put her to bed myself.'

'Leave her with me for tomorrow, Beatrice, and write me your address on this leaf of my pocketbook. In the evening I will bring her home to you – and to her father.'

* * *

'Hallo!' cried Polly, putting her saucy sunny face in at the door next morning when breakfast was ready: 'I thought I was fetched last night?'

'So you were, Polly, but I asked leave to keep you here for the day, and to take you home in the evening.'

'Upon my word!' said Polly. 'You are very cool, ain't you?'

However, Polly seemed to think it a good idea, and added: 'I suppose I must give you a kiss, though you *are* cool.' The kiss given and taken, they sat down to breakfast in a highly conversational tone.

'Of course, you are going to amuse me?' said Polly.

'Oh, of course!' said Barbox Brothers.

In the pleasurable height of her anticipations, Polly found it indispensable to put down her piece of toast, cross one of her little fat knees over the other, and bring her little fat right hand down into her left hand with a businesslike slap. After this gathering of herself together, Polly, by that time a mere heap of dimples, asked in a wheedling manner: 'What are we going to do, you dear old thing?'

'Why, I was thinking,' said Barbox Brothers, 'but are you fond of horses, Polly?'

'Ponies, I am,' said Polly, 'especially when their tails are long. But horses – n-no – too big, you know.'

'Well,' pursued Barbox Brothers, in a spirit of grave mysterious confidence adapted to the importance of the consultation, 'I did see yesterday, Polly, on the walls, pictures of two long-tailed ponies, speckled all over –'

'No, no, *no!*' cried Polly, in an ecstatic desire to linger on the charming details. 'Not speckled all over!'

'Speckled all over. Which ponies jump through hoops –'

'No, no, *no!*' cried Polly as before. 'They never jump through hoops!'

'Yes, they do. Oh, I assure you they do! And eat pie in pinafores –'

'Ponies eating pie in pinafores!' said Polly. 'What a storyteller you are, ain't you?'

'Upon my honour – and fire off guns.'

(Polly hardly seemed to see the force of the ponies resorting to firearms.)

'And I was thinking,' pursued the exemplary Barbox, 'that if you and I were to go to the circus where these ponies are, it would do our constitutions good.'

'Does that mean amuse us?' inquired Polly. 'What long words you do use, don't you?'

Apologetic for having wandered out of his depth, he replied: 'That means amuse us. That is exactly what it means. There are many other wonders besides the ponies, and we shall see them all. Ladies and gentlemen in spangled dresses, and elephants and lions and tigers.'

Polly became observant of the teapot, with a curled-up nose indicating some uneasiness of mind. 'They never get out, of course,' she remarked as a mere truism.

'The elephants and lions and tigers? Oh, dear no!'

'Oh dear no!' said Polly. 'And of course nobody's afraid of the ponies shooting anybody.'

'Not the least in the world.'

'No, no, not the least in the world,' said Polly.

'I was also thinking,' proceeded Barbox, 'that if we were to look in at the toy shop, to choose a doll –'

'Not dressed!' cried Polly with a clap of her hands. 'No, no, *no*, not dressed!'

'Full dressed. Together with a house, and all things necessary for housekeeping –'

Polly gave a little scream, and seemed in danger of falling into a swoon of bliss. 'What a darling you are!' she languidly exclaimed, leaning back in her chair. 'Come and be hugged, or I must come and hug you.'

This resplendent programme was carried into execution with the utmost rigour of the law. It being essential to make the purchase of the doll its first feature – or that lady would have lost the ponies – the toy shop expedition took precedence. Polly in the magic warehouse, with a doll as large as herself under each arm, and a neat assortment of some twenty more on view upon the counter, did indeed present a spectacle of indecision not quite compatible with unalloyed happiness – but the light cloud passed. The lovely specimen oftenest chosen, oftenest rejected, and finally abided by, was of Circassian descent, possessing as much boldness of beauty as was reconcilable with extreme feebleness of mouth, and combining a sky-blue silk pelisse with rose-coloured satin trousers, and a black velvet hat: which this fair stranger to our northern shores would seem to have founded on the portraits of the late Duchess of Kent. The name this distinguished foreigner brought with her from beneath the glowing skies of a sunny clime was (on Polly's authority) Miss Melluka, and the costly nature of her outfit as a housekeeper, from the Barbox coffers, may be inferred from the two facts that her silver teaspoons were as large as her kitchen poker, and that the proportions of her watch exceeded those of her frying pan. Miss Melluka was graciously pleased to express her entire approbation of the circus, and so was Polly; for the ponies *were* speckled, and brought down nobody when they fired, and the savagery of the wild beasts appeared to be mere smoke – which article, in fact, they did produce in large quantities from their insides. The Barbox absorption in the general subject throughout the realisation of these delights was again a sight to see, nor was it less worthy to behold at dinner, when he drank to Miss Melluka, tied stiff in a chair opposite to Polly (the fair Circassian possessing an unbendable spine), and even induced the waiter to assist in carrying out with due decorum the prevailing glorious idea. To wind up, there came the agreeable fever of getting Miss Melluka and all her wardrobe and rich possessions into a fly with Polly, to be taken home. But, by that time, Polly had become unable to look upon such accumulated joys with waking eyes, and had withdrawn her consciousness into the wonderful paradise of a child's sleep. 'Sleep, Polly, sleep,' said Barbox Brothers, as her head dropped on his shoulder; 'you shall not fall out of this bed easily, at any rate!'

What rustling piece of paper he took from his pocket, and carefully folded into the bosom of Polly's frock, shall not be mentioned. He said nothing about it, and nothing shall be said about it. They drove to a modest suburb of the great ingenious town, and stopped at the forecourt of a small house. 'Do not wake the child,' said Barbox Brothers softly to the driver, 'I will carry her in as she is.'

Greeting the light at the opened door which was held by Polly's mother, Polly's bearer passed on with mother and child into a ground-floor room. There, stretched on a sofa, lay a sick man, sorely wasted, who covered his eyes with his emaciated hands.

'Tresham,' said Barbox, in a kindly voice, 'I have brought you back your Polly, fast asleep. Give me your hand, and tell me you are better.'

The sick man reached forth his right hand, and bowed his head over the hand into which it was taken, and kissed it. 'Thank you, thank you! I may say that I am well and happy.'

'That's brave,' said Barbox. 'Tresham, I have a fancy – can you make room for me beside you here?'

He sat down on the sofa as he said the words, cherishing the plump peachy cheek that lay uppermost on his shoulder.

'I have a fancy, Tresham (I am getting quite an old fellow now, you know, and old fellows may take fancies into their heads sometimes), to

41

give up Polly, having found her, to no one but you. Will you take her from me?'

As the father held out his arms for the child, each of the two men looked steadily at the other.

'She is very dear to you, Tresham?'

'Unutterably dear.'

'God bless her! It is not much, Polly,' he continued, turning his eyes upon her peaceful face as he apostrophised her, 'it is not much, Polly, for a blind and sinful man to invoke a blessing on something so far better than himself as a little child is; but it would be much – much upon his cruel head, and much upon his guilty soul – if he could be so wicked as to invoke a curse. He had better have a millstone round his neck, and be cast into the deepest sea. Live and thrive, my pretty baby!' Here he kissed her. 'Live and prosper, and become in time the mother of other little children, like the angels who behold the Father's face!'

He kissed her again, gave her up gently to both her parents, and went out.

But he went not to Wales. No, he never went to Wales. He went straightway for another stroll about the town, and he looked in upon the people at their work, and at their play, here, there, everywhere and where not. For he was Barbox Brothers and Co. now, and had taken thousands of partners into the solitary firm.

He had at length got back to his hotel room, and was standing before his fire refreshing himself with a glass of hot drink which he had stood upon the chimney piece, when he heard the town clocks striking and, referring to his watch, found the evening to have so slipped away that they were striking twelve. As he put up his watch again, his eyes met those of his reflection in the chimney-glass.

'Why, it's your birthday already,' he said, smiling. 'You are looking very well. I wish you many happy returns of the day.'

He had never before bestowed that wish upon himself. 'By Jupiter,' he discovered, 'it alters the whole case of running away from one's birthday! It's a thing to explain to Phoebe. Besides, here is quite a long story to tell her, that has sprung out of the road with no story. I'll go back, instead of going on. I'll go back by my friend Lamps's Up X presently.'

He went back to Mugby Junction, and in point of fact he established himself at Mugby Junction. It was the convenient place to live in for brightening Phoebe's life. It was the convenient place to live in for having her taught music by Beatrice. It was the convenient place to live in for occasionally borrowing Polly. It was the convenient place to live in for being joined at will to all sorts of agreeable places and persons. So he became settled there and, his house standing in an elevated situation, it is noteworthy of him in conclusion, as Polly herself might (not irreverently) have put it:

> *There was an Old Barbox who lived on a hill,*
> *And if he ain't gone, he lives there still.*

HERE FOLLOWS THE SUBSTANCE OF WHAT WAS SEEN, HEARD, OR OTHERWISE PICKED UP BY THE GENTLEMAN FOR NOWHERE IN HIS CAREFUL STUDY OF THE JUNCTION.

MAIN LINE. THE BOY AT MUGBY
[by Charles Dickens]

I am the Boy at Mugby. That's about what *I* am.

You don't know what I mean? What a pity! But I think you do. I think you must. Look here. I am the Boy at what is called The Refreshment Room at Mugby Junction, and what's proudest boast is, that it never yet refreshed a mortal being.

Up in a corner of the Down Refreshment Room at Mugby Junction, in the height of twenty-seven cross-draughts (I've often counted 'em while they brush the First-Class hair twenty-seven ways), behind the bottles, among the glasses, bounded on the nor'west by the beer, stood pretty far to the right of a metallic object that's at times the tea urn and at times the soup tureen – according to the nature of the last twang imparted to its contents which are the same groundwork – fended off from the traveller by a barrier of stale sponge cakes erected atop of the counter, and lastly exposed sideways to the glare of Our Missis' eye – you ask a Boy so sitiwated, next time you stop in a hurry at Mugby, for anything to drink – you take particular notice that he'll try to seem not to hear you, that he'll appear in a absent manner to survey the Line through a transparent medium composed of your head and body, and that he won't serve you as long as you can possibly bear it. That's Me.

What a lark it is! We are the Model Establishment, we are, at Mugby. Other Refreshment Rooms send their imperfect young ladies up to be finished off by Our Missis. For some of the young ladies, when they're new to the business, come into it mild! Ah! Our Missis, she soon takes that out of 'em. Why, I originally come into the business meek myself. But Our Missis, she soon took that out of *me*.

What a delightful lark it is! I look upon us Refreshmenters as ockipying the only proudly independent footing on the Line. There's Papers for instance – my honourable friend, if he will allow me to call him so – him as belongs to Smith's bookstall. Why, he no more dares to be up to our Refreshmenting games than he dares to jump atop of a locomotive with her steam at full pressure, and cut away upon her alone, driving himself, at limited-mail speed. Papers, he'd get his head punched at every compartment, first, second and third, the whole length of a train, if he was to ventur to imitate my demeanour. It's the same with the porters, the same with the guards, the same with the ticket clerks, the same the whole way up to the secretary, traffic manager, or very chairman. There ain't a one among 'em on the nobly independent footing we are. Did you ever catch one of *them*, when you wanted anything of him, making a system of surveying the Line through a transparent medium composed of your head and body? I should hope not.

You should see our Bandolining Room at Mugby Junction. It's led to by the door behind the counter, which you'll notice usually stands ajar, and it's the room where Our Missis and our young ladies Bandolines their hair. You should see 'em at it, betwixt trains, Bandolining away, as if they was anointing themselves for the combat. When you're telegraphed, you should see their noses all a-going up with scorn, as if it was a part of the working of the same Cooke and Wheatstone electrical machinery. You should hear Our Missis give the word, 'Here comes the Beast to be Fed!' and then you should see 'em indignantly skipping across the Line, from the Up to the Down, or Wicer Warsaw, and begin to pitch the stale pastry into the plates, and chuck the sawdust sangwiches under the glass covers, and get out the – ha ha ha! – the sherry – oh my eye, my eye! – for your Refreshment.

It's only in the Isle of the Brave and Land of the Free (by which, of course, I mean to say Britannia) that Refreshmenting is so effective, so 'olesome, so constitutional a check upon the public. There was a Foreigner, which having politely, with his hat off, beseeched our young ladies and Our Missis for 'a leetel gloss host prarndee', and having had the Line surveyed through him by all and no other acknowledgment, was a-proceeding at last to help himself, as seems to be the custom in his own country, when Our Missis, with her hair almost a-coming un-Bandolined with rage, and her eyes omitting sparks, flew at him, cotched the decanter out of his hand, and said: 'Put it down! I won't allow that!' The foreigner turned pale, stepped back with his arms stretched out in front of him, his hands clasped and his shoulders riz, and exclaimed: 'Ah! Is it possible this! That these disdaineous females and this ferocious old woman are placed here by the administration, not only to empoison the voyagers, but to affront them! Great heaven! How arrives it? The English people. Or is he then a slave? Or idiot?' Another time, a merry, wide-awake American gent had tried the sawdust and spit it out, and had tried the Sherry and spit that out, and had tried in vain to sustain exhausted natur upon Butterscotch, and had been rather extra Bandolined and Line-surveyed through, when, as the bell was ringing and he paid Our Missis, he says, very loud and good-tempered: 'I tell Yew what 'tis, ma'arm. I la'af. Theer! I la'af. I Dew. I oughter ha' seen most things, for I hail from the Onlimited side of the Atlantic Ocean, and I haive travelled right slick over the Limited, head on through Jee-rusalemm and the East, and likeways France and Italy, Europe Old World, and am now upon the track to the Chief Europian Village; but such an Institution as Yew, and Yewer young ladies, and Yewer fixin's solid and liquid, afore the glorious Tarnal,[1] I never did see yet! And if I hain't found the eighth wonder of monarchical Creation, in finding Yew, and Yewer young ladies, and Yewer fixin's solid and liquid, all as aforesaid, established in a country where the people air not absolute Loo-naticks, I am Extra Double Darned with a Nip and Frizzle to the innermostest grit! Wheerfur – Theer! – I la'af! I Dew, ma'arm. I la'af!' And so he went, stamping and shaking his sides, along the platform all the way to his own compartment.

I think it was her standing up agin the Foreigner as giv' Our Missis the idea of going over to France, and droring a comparison betwixt Refreshmenting as followed among the frog-eaters and Refreshmenting as triumphant in the Isle of the Brave and Land of the Free (by which of course I mean to say agin, Britannia). Our young ladies, Miss Whiff, Miss Piff, and Mrs Sniff, was unanimous opposed to her going; for, as they says to Our Missis one and all, it is well beknown to the hends of the herth as no other nation except Britain has a idea of anythink, but above all of business. Why then should you tire yourself to prove what is already proved? Our Missis however (being a teaser at all pints) stood out grim obstinate, and got a return pass by Southeastern Tidal, to go right through, if such should be her dispositions, to Marseilles.

Sniff is husband to Mrs Sniff, and is a regular insignificant cove. He looks arter the sawdust department in a back room, and is some-times, when we are very hard put to it, let behind the counter with a corkscrew; but never when it can be helped, his demeanour towards the public being disgusting servile. How Mrs Sniff ever come so far to lower herself as to marry him, I don't know; but I suppose *he* does, and I should think he wished he didn't, for he leads a awful life. Mrs Sniff couldn't be much harder with him if he was public. Similarly, Miss Whiff and Miss Piff, taking the tone of Mrs Sniff, they shoulder Sniff about when he *is* let in with a corkscrew, and they whisk things out of his hands when in his servility he is a-going to let the public have 'em, and they snap him up when in the crawling baseness of his spirit he is a-going to answer a public question, and they drore more tears into his eyes than ever the mustard does which he all day long lays on to the sawdust. (But it ain't strong.) Once, when Sniff had the repulsiveness to reach across to get the milk pot to hand over for a baby, I see Our Missis in her rage catch him by both his shoulders, and spin him out into the Bandolining Room.

But Mrs Sniff – how different! She's the one! She's the one as you'll notice to be always looking another way from you, when you look at her. She's the one with the small waist buckled in tight in front, and with the lace cuffs at her wrists, which she puts on the edge of the counter before her, and stands a-smoothing while the public foams. This smoothing the cuffs and looking another way while the public foams is the last accomplishment taught to the young ladies as come to Mugby to be finished by Our Missis; and it's always taught by Mrs Sniff.

When Our Missis went away upon her journey, Mrs Sniff was left in charge. She did hold the public in check most beautiful! In all my time, I never see half so many cups of tea given without milk to people as wanted it with, nor half so many cups of tea with milk given to people as wanted it without. When foaming ensued, Mrs Sniff would say: 'Then you'd better settle it among yourselves, and change with one another.' It was a most highly delicious lark. I enjoyed the Refreshmenting business more than ever, and was so glad I had took to it when young.

Our Missis returned. It got circulated among the young ladies, and it as it might be penetrated to me through the crevices of the Bandolining Room, that she had Orrors to reveal, if revelations so contemptible could be dignified with the name. Agitation become awakened. Excitement was up in the stirrups. Expectation stood a-tiptoe. At length it was put forth that on our slackest evening in the week, and at our slackest time of that evening betwixt trains, Our Missis would give her views of foreign Refreshmenting, in the Bandolining Room.

It was arranged tasteful for the purpose. The Bandolining table and glass was hid in a corner, a armchair was elevated on a packing case for Our Missis' ockypation, a table and a tumbler of water (no sherry in it, thankee) was placed beside it. Two of the pupils, the season being autumn, and hollyhocks and dahlias being in, ornamented the wall with three devices in those flowers. On one might be read, '*May Albion Never Learn*'; on another '*Keep the Public Down*'; on another, '*Our Refreshmenting Charter*'. The whole had a beautiful appearance, with which the beauty of the sentiments corresponded.

On Our Missis' brow was wrote Severity, as she ascended the fatal platform. (Not that that was anythink new.) Miss Whiff and Miss Piff sat at her feet. Three chairs from the Waiting Room might have been perceived by a average eye, in front of her, on which the pupils was accommodated. Behind them a very close observer might have discerned a Boy. Myself.

'Where,' said Our Missis, glancing gloomily around, 'is Sniff?'

'I thought it better,' answered Mrs Sniff, 'that he should not be let to come in. He is such an Ass.'

'No doubt,' assented Our Missis. 'But for that reason is it not desirable to improve his mind?'

'Oh, nothing will ever improve *him*,' said Mrs Sniff.

'However,' pursued Our Missis, 'call him in, Ezekiel.'

I called him in. The appearance of the low-minded cove was hailed with disapprobation from all sides, on account of his having brought his corkscrew with him. He pleaded 'the force of habit'.

'The force!' said Mrs Sniff. 'Don't let us have you talking about force, for Gracious' sake. There! Do stand still where you are, with your back against the wall.'

He is a smiling piece of vacancy, and he smiled in the mean way in which he will even smile at the public if he gets a chance (language can say no meaner of him), and he stood upright near the door with the back of his head agin the wall, as if he was a-waiting for somebody to come and measure his heighth for the Army.

'I should not enter, ladies,' says Our Missis, 'on the revolting disclosures I am about to make, if it was not in the hope that they will cause you to be yet more implacable in the exercise of the power you wield in a constitutional country, and yet more devoted to the constitutional motto which I see before me,' – it was behind her, but the words sounded better so – ' "May Albion never learn!" '

Here the pupils as had made the motto admired it, and cried, 'Hear! Hear! Hear!' Sniff, showing an inclination to join in chorus, got himself frowned down by every brow.

'The baseness of the French,' pursued Our Missis, 'as displayed in the fawning nature of their Refreshmenting, equals, if not surpasses, anythink as was ever heard of the baseness of the celebrated Bonaparte.'

Miss Whiff, Miss Piff, and me, we drored a heavy breath, equal to saying, 'We thought as much!' Miss Whiff and Miss Piff seeming to object to my droring mine along with theirs, I drored another to aggravate 'em.

'Shall I be believed,' says Our Missis, with flashing eyes, 'when I tell you that no sooner had I set my foot upon that treacherous shore –'

Here Sniff, either bursting out mad, or thinking aloud, says, in a low voice: 'Feet. Plural, you know.'

The cowering that come upon him when he was spurned by all eyes, added to his being beneath contempt, was sufficient punishment for a cove so grovelling. In the midst of a silence rendered more impressive by the turned-up female noses with which it was pervaded, Our Missis went on:

'Shall I be believed when I tell you that no sooner had I landed,' this word with a killing look at Sniff, 'on that treacherous shore, than I was ushered into a Refreshment Room where there were – I do not exaggerate – actually eatable things to eat?'

A groan burst from the ladies. I not only did myself the honour of jining, but also of lengthening it out.

'Where there were,' Our Missis added, 'not only eatable things to eat, but also drinkable things to drink?'

A murmur, swelling almost into a scream, ariz. Miss Piff, trembling with indignation, called out, 'Name!'

'I *will* name,' said Our Missis. 'There was roast fowls, hot and cold; there was smoking roast veal surrounded with browned potatoes; there was hot soup with (again, I ask, shall I be credited?) nothing bitter in it, and no flour to choke off the consumer; there was a variety of cold dishes set off with jelly; there was salad; there was – mark me! – *fresh* pastry, and that of a light construction; there was a luscious show of fruit. There was bottles and decanters of sound small wine, of every size and adapted to every pocket; the same odious statement will apply to brandy; and these were set out upon the counter so that all could help themselves.'

Our Missis' lips so quivered that Mrs Sniff, though scarcely less convulsed than she were, got up and held the tumbler to them.

'This,' proceeds Our Missis, 'was my first unconstitutional experience. Well would it have been, if it had been my last and worst. But no. As I proceeded further into that enslaved and ignorant land, its aspect became more hideous. I need not explain to this assembly the ingredients and formation of the British Refreshment sangwich?'

Universal laughter – except from Sniff, who, as sangwich-cutter, shook his head in a state of the utmost dejection as he stood with it agin the wall.

'Well!' said Our Missis, with dilated nostrils. 'Take a fresh, crisp, long, crusty penny loaf made of the whitest and best flour. Cut it longwise through the middle. Insert a fair and nicely fitting slice of ham. Tie a smart piece of ribbon round the middle of the whole to bind it together. Add at one end a neat wrapper of clean white paper by which to hold it. And the universal French Refreshment sangwich busts on your disgusted vision.'

A cry of 'Shame!' from all – except Sniff, which rubbed his stomach with a soothing hand.

'I need not,' said Our Missis, 'explain to this assembly the usual formation and fitting of the British Refreshment Room?'

No, no, and laughter. Sniff agin shaking his head in low spirits agin the wall.

'Well,' said Our Missis, 'what would you say to a general decoration of everythink, to hangings (sometimes elegant), to easy velvet furniture, to abundance of little tables, to abundance of little seats, to brisk bright waiters, to great convenience, to a pervading cleanliness and taste-fulness positively addressing the public, and making the Beast thinking itself worth the pains?'

Contemptuous fury on the part of all the ladies. Mrs Sniff looking as if she wanted somebody to hold her, and everybody else looking as if they'd rayther not.

'Three times,' said Our Missis, working herself into a truly terrimenjious state, 'three times did I see these shamful things, only between the coast and Paris, and not counting either: at Hazebroucke, at Arras, at Amiens. But worse remains. Tell me, what would you call a person who should propose in England that there should be kept, say at our own model Mugby Junction, pretty baskets, each holding an assorted cold lunch and dessert for one, each at a certain fixed price, and each within a passenger's power to take away, to empty in the carriage at perfect leisure, and to return at another station fifty or a hundred miles further on?'

There was disagreement what such a person should be called. Whether revolutionist, atheist, Bright (*I* said him), or un-English. Miss Piff screeched her shrill opinion last, in the words: 'A malignant maniac!'

'I adopt,' says Our Missis, 'the brand set upon such a person by the righteous indignation of my friend Miss Piff. A malignant maniac. Know then, that that malignant maniac has sprung from the congenial soil of France, and that his malignant madness was in unchecked action on this same part of my journey.'

I noticed that Sniff was a-rubbing his hands, and that Mrs Sniff had got her eye upon him. But I did not take more particular notice, owing to the excited state in which the young ladies was, and to feeling myself called upon to keep it up with a howl.

'On my experience south of Paris,' said Our Missis, in a deep tone, 'I will not expatiate. Too loathsome were the task! But fancy this. Fancy a guard coming round, with the train at full speed, to enquire how many for dinner. Fancy his telegraphing forward the number of dinners. Fancy every one expected, and the table elegantly laid for the complete party. Fancy a charming dinner, in a charming room, and the head cook, concerned for the honour of every dish, superintending in his clean white jacket and cap. Fancy the Beast travelling six hundred miles on end, very fast, and with great punctuality, yet being taught to expect all this to be done for it!'

A spirited chorus of 'The Beast!'

I noticed that Sniff was agin a-rubbing his stomach with a soothing hand, and that he had drored up one leg. But agin I didn't take particular notice, looking on myself as called upon to stimilate public feeling. It being a lark besides.

'Putting everything together,' said Our Missis, 'French Refreshmenting comes to this, and oh it comes to a nice total! First: eatable things to eat, and drinkable things to drink.'

A groan from the young ladies, kep' up by me.

'Second: convenience, and even elegance.'

Another groan from the young ladies, kep' up by me.

'Third: moderate charges.'

This time a groan from me, kep' up by the young ladies.

'Fourth – and here,' says Our Missis, 'I claim your angriest sympathy – attention, common civility, nay, even politeness!'

Me and the young ladies regularly raging mad all together.

'And I cannot in conclusion,' says Our Missis, with her spitefullest sneer, 'give you a completer pictur of that despicable nation (after what I have related) than assuring you that they wouldn't bear our constitutional ways and noble independence at Mugby Junction, for a single month, and that they would turn us to the right about and put another system in our places, as soon as look at us; perhaps sooner, for I do not believe they have the good taste to care to look at us twice.'

The swelling tumult was arrested in its rise. Sniff, bore away by his servile disposition, had drored up his leg with a higher and a higher relish, and was now discovered to be waving his corkscrew over his head. It was at this moment that Mrs Sniff, who had kep' her eye upon him like the fabled obelisk,[2] descended on her victim. Our Missis followed them both out, and cries was heard in the sawdust department.

You come into the Down Refreshment Room, at the Junction, making believe you don't know me, and I'll pint you out with my right thumb over my shoulder which is Our Missis, and which is Miss Whiff, and which is Miss Piff, and which is Mrs Sniff. But you won't get a chance to see Sniff, because he disappeared that night. Whether he perished, tore to pieces, I cannot say; but his corkscrew alone remains, to bear witness to the servility of his disposition.

No. 1 BRANCH LINE. THE SIGNALMAN
[by Charles Dickens]

'Halloa! Below there!'

When he heard a voice thus calling to him, he was standing at the door of his box, with a flag in his hand, furled round its short pole. One would have thought, considering the nature of the ground, that he could not have doubted from what quarter the voice came; but, instead of looking up to where I stood on the top of the steep cutting nearly over his head, he turned himself about and looked down the line. There was something remarkable in his manner of doing so, though I could not have said, for my life, what. But I know it was remarkable enough to attract my notice, even though his figure was foreshortened and shadowed, down in the deep trench, and mine was high above him, so steeped in the glow of an angry sunset that I had shaded my eyes with my hand before I saw him at all.

'Halloa! Below!'

From looking down the line, he turned himself about again and, raising his eyes, saw my figure high above him.

'Is there any path by which I can come down and speak to you?'

He looked up at me without replying, and I looked down at him without pressing him too soon with a repetition of my idle question. Just then, there came a vague vibration in the earth and air, quickly changing into a violent pulsation, and an oncoming rush that caused me to start back, as though it had force to draw me down. When such vapour as rose to my height from this rapid train had passed me and was skimming away over the landscape, I looked down again, and saw him refurling the flag he had shown while the train went by.

I repeated my enquiry. After a pause, during which he seemed to regard me with fixed attention, he motioned with his rolled-up flag towards a point on my level, some two or three hundred yards distant. I called down to him, 'All right!' and made for that point. There, by dint of looking closely about me, I found a rough zigzag descending path notched out: which I followed.

The cutting was extremely deep, and unusually precipitate. It was made through a clammy stone that became oozier and wetter as I went down. For these reasons, I found the way long enough to give me time to recall a singular air of reluctance or compulsion with which he had pointed out the path.

When I came down low enough upon the zigzag descent, to see him again, I saw that he was standing between the rails on the way by which the train had lately passed, in an attitude as if he were waiting for me to appear. He had his left hand at his chin, and that left elbow rested on his right hand crossed over his breast. His attitude was one of such expectation and watchfulness that I stopped a moment, wondering at it.

I resumed my downward way and, stepping out upon the level of the railroad and drawing nearer to him, saw that he was a dark sallow man, with a dark beard and rather heavy eyebrows. His post was in as solitary and dismal a place as ever I saw. On either side, a dripping-wet wall of jagged stone, excluding all view but a strip of sky – the perspective one way, only a crooked prolongation of this great dungeon; the shorter perspective in the other direction, terminating in a gloomy red light, and the gloomier entrance to a black tunnel, in whose massive architecture there was a barbarous, depressing and forbidding air. So little sunlight ever found its way to this spot that it had an earthy deadly smell; and so much cold wind rushed through it that it struck chill to me, as if I had left the natural world.

Before he stirred, I was near enough to him to have touched him. Not even then removing his eyes from mine, he stepped back one step, and lifted his hand.

This was a lonesome post to occupy (I said), and it had riveted my attention when I looked down from up yonder. A visitor was a rarity, I should suppose – not an unwelcome rarity, I hoped. In me, he merely saw a man who had been shut up within narrow limits all his life, and who, being at last set free, had a newly awakened interest in these great works. To such purpose I spoke to him; but I am far from sure of the terms I used, for, besides that I am not happy in opening any conversation, there was something in the man that daunted me.

He directed a most curious look towards the red light near the tunnel's mouth, and looked all about it, as if something were missing from it, and then looked at me.

That light was part of his charge, was it not?

He answered in a low voice: 'Don't you know it is?'

The monstrous thought came into my mind, as I perused the fixed eyes and the saturnine face, that this was a spirit, not a man. I have speculated since, whether there may have been infection in his mind.

In my turn, I stepped back. But in making the action, I detected in his eyes some latent fear of me. This put the monstrous thought to flight.

'You look at me,' I said, forcing a smile, 'as if you had a dread of me.'

'I was doubtful,' he returned, 'whether I had seen you before.'

'Where?'

He pointed to the red light he had looked at.

'There?' I said.

Intently watchful of me, he replied (but without sound), 'Yes.'

'My good fellow, what should I do there? However, be that as it may, I never was there, you may swear.'

'I think I may,' he rejoined. 'Yes. I am sure I may.'

His manner cleared, like my own. He replied to my remarks with readiness, and in well-chosen words. Had he much to do there? Yes – that was to say, he had enough responsibility to bear; but exactness and watchfulness were what was required of him, and of actual work – manual labour – he had next to none. To change that signal, to trim those lights and to turn this iron handle now and then was all he had to do under that head. Regarding those many long and lonely hours of which I seemed to make so much, he could only say that the routine of his life had shaped itself into that form, and he had grown used to it. He had taught himself a language down here – if only to know it by sight and to have formed his own crude ideas of its pronunciation could be called learning it. He had also worked at fractions and decimals, and tried a little algebra; but he was, and had been as a boy, a poor hand at figures. Was it necessary for him when on duty always to remain in that channel of damp air, and could he never rise into the sunshine from between those high stone walls? Why, that depended upon times and circumstances. Under some conditions there would be less upon the line than under others, and the same held good as to certain hours of the day and night. In bright weather, he did choose occasions for getting a little above these lower shadows; but, being at all times liable to be called by his electric bell, and at such times listening for it with redoubled anxiety, the relief was less than I would suppose.

He took me into his box, where there was a fire, a desk for an official book in which he had to make certain entries, a telegraphic instrument with its dial face and needles, and the little bell of which he had spoken. On my trusting that he would excuse the remark that he had been well educated, and (I hoped I might say without offence) perhaps educated above that station, he observed that instances of slight incongruity in such wise would rarely be found wanting among large bodies of men; that he had heard it was so in workhouses, in the police force, even in that last desperate resource, the army; and that he knew it was so, more or less, in any great railway staff. He had been, when young (if I could believe it, sitting in that hut – he scarcely could), a student of natural philosophy, and had attended lectures; but he had run wild, misused his opportunities, gone down, and never risen again. He had no complaint to offer about that. He had made his bed and he lay upon it. It was far too late to make another.

All that I have here condensed he said in a quiet manner, with his grave dark regards divided between me and the fire. He threw in the word 'sir' from time to time, and especially when he referred to his youth, as though to request me to understand that he claimed to be nothing but what I found him. He was several times interrupted by the little bell, and had to read off messages and send replies. Once, he had to stand without the door and display a flag as a train passed, and make some verbal communication to the driver. In the discharge of his duties I observed him to be remarkably exact and vigilant, breaking off his discourse at a syllable, and remaining silent until what he had to do was done.

In a word, I should have set this man down as one of the safest of men to be employed in that capacity, but for the circumstance that while he was speaking to me he twice broke off with a fallen colour, turned his face towards the little bell when it did NOT ring, opened the door of the hut (which was kept shut to exclude the unhealthy damp) and looked out towards the red light near the mouth of the tunnel. On both of those occasions, he came back to the fire with the inexplicable air upon him which I had remarked, without being able to define, when we were so far asunder.

Said I when I rose to leave him: 'You almost make me think that I have met with a contented man.'

(I am afraid I must acknowledge that I said it to lead him on.)

'I believe I used to be so,' he rejoined, in the low voice in which he had first spoken; 'but I am troubled, sir, I am troubled.'

He would have recalled the words if he could. He had said them, however, and I took them up quickly.

'With what? What is your trouble?'

'It is very difficult to impart, sir. It is very, very difficult to speak of. If ever you make me another visit, I will try to tell you.'

'But I expressly intend to make you another visit. Say, when shall it be?'

'I go off early in the morning, and I shall be on again at ten tomorrow night, sir.'

'I will come at eleven.'

He thanked me, and went out at the door with me. 'I'll show my white light, sir,' he said, in his peculiar low voice, ''till you have found the way up. When you have found it, don't call out! And when you are at the top, don't call out!'

His manner seemed to make the place strike colder to me, but I said no more than, 'Very well.'

'And when you come down tomorrow night, don't call out! Let me ask you a parting question. What made you cry "Halloa! Below there!" tonight?'

'Heaven knows,' said I. 'I cried something to that effect –'

'Not to that effect, sir. Those were the very words. I know them well.'

'Admit those were the very words. I said them, no doubt, because I saw you below.'

'For no other reason?'

'What other reason could I possibly have!'

'You had no feeling that they were conveyed to you in any super-natural way?'

'No.'

He wished me goodnight, and held up his light. I walked by the side of the down line of rails (with a very disagreeable sensation of a train coming behind me), until I found the path. It was easier to mount than to descend, and I got back to my inn without any adventure.

Punctual to my appointment, I placed my foot on the first notch of the zigzag next night, as the distant clocks were striking eleven. He was waiting for me at the bottom, with his white light on.

'I have not called out,' I said, when we came close together; 'may I speak now?'

'By all means, sir.'

'Goodnight then, and here's my hand.'

'Goodnight, sir, and here's mine.'

With that, we walked side by side to his box, entered it, closed the door, and sat down by the fire.

'I have made up my mind, sir,' he began, bending forward as soon as we were seated, and speaking in a tone but a little above a whisper, 'that you shall not have to ask me twice what troubles me. I took you for someone else yesterday evening. That troubles me.'

'That mistake?'

'No. That someone else.'

'Who is it?'

'I don't know.'

'Like me?'

'I don't know. I never saw the face. The left arm is across the face, and the right arm is waved. Violently waved. This way.'

I followed his action with my eyes, and it was the action of an arm gesticulating with the utmost passion and vehemence: 'For God's sake clear the way!'

'One moonlight night,' said the man, 'I was sitting here, when I heard a voice cry, "Halloa! Below there!" I started up, looked from that door, and saw this someone else standing by the red light near the tunnel, waving as I just now showed you. The voice seemed hoarse with shouting, and it cried, "Look out! Look out!" And then again "Halloa! Below there! Look out!" I caught up my lamp, turned it on red, and ran towards the figure, calling, "What's wrong? What has happened? Where?" It stood just outside the blackness of the tunnel. I advanced so close upon it that I wondered at its keeping the sleeve across its eyes. I ran right up at it, and had my hand stretched out to pull the sleeve away, when it was gone.'

'Into the tunnel,' said I.

'No. I ran on into the tunnel, five hundred yards. I stopped and held my lamp above my head, and saw the figures of the measured distance, and saw the wet stains stealing down the walls and trickling through the arch. I ran out again, faster than I had run in (for I had a mortal abhorrence of the place upon me), and I looked all round the red light with my own red light, and I went up the iron ladder to the gallery atop of it, and I came down again, and ran back here. I telegraphed both ways, "An alarm has been given. Is anything wrong?" The answer came back, both ways: "All well."'

Resisting the slow touch of a frozen finger tracing out my spine, I showed him how that this figure must be a deception of his sense of sight, and how that figures, originating in disease of the delicate nerves that minister to the functions of the eye, were known to have often troubled patients, some of whom had become conscious of the nature of their affliction, and had even proved it by experiments upon themselves. 'As to an imaginary cry,' said I, 'do but listen for a moment to the wind in this unnatural valley while we speak so low, and to the wild harp it makes of the telegraph wires!'

That was all very well, he returned, after we had sat listening for a while, and he ought to know something of the wind and the wires, he who so often passed long winter nights there, alone and watching. But he would beg to remark that he had not finished.

I asked his pardon, and he slowly added these words, touching my arm: 'Within six hours after the appearance, the memorable accident on this line happened, and within ten hours the dead and wounded were brought along through the tunnel over the spot where the figure had stood.'

A disagreeable shudder crept over me, but I did my best against it. It was not to be denied, I rejoined, that this was a remarkable coincidence, calculated deeply to impress his mind. But it was unquestionable that remarkable coincidences did continually occur, and they must be taken into account in dealing with such a subject. Though to be sure I must admit, I added (for I thought I saw that he was going to bring the objection to bear upon me), men of common sense did not allow much for coincidences in making the ordinary calculations of life.

He again begged to remark that he had not finished.

I again begged his pardon for being betrayed into interruptions.

'This,' he said, again laying his hand upon my arm, and glancing over his shoulder with hollow eyes, 'was just a year ago. Six or seven months passed, and I had recovered from the surprise and shock, when one morning, as the day was breaking, I, standing at that door, looked towards the red light, and saw the spectre again.' He stopped, with a fixed look at me.

'Did it cry out?'

'No. It was silent.'

'Did it wave its arm?'

'No. It leant against the shaft of the light, with both hands before the face. Like this.'

Once more, I followed his action with my eyes. It was an action of mourning. I have seen such an attitude in stone figures on tombs.

'Did you go up to it?'

'I came in and sat down, partly to collect my thoughts, partly because it had turned me faint. When I went to the door again, daylight was above me, and the ghost was gone.'

'But nothing followed? Nothing came of this?'

He touched me on the arm with his forefinger twice or thrice, giving a ghastly nod each time:

'That very day, as a train came out of the tunnel, I noticed, at a carriage window on my side, what looked like a confusion of hands and heads, and something waved. I saw it, just in time to signal the driver, "Stop!" He shut off, and put his brake on, but the train drifted past here a hundred and fifty yards or more. I ran after it and, as I went along, heard terrible screams and cries. A beautiful young lady had died instantaneously in one of the compartments and was brought in here, and laid down on this floor between us.'

Involuntarily, I pushed my chair back, as I looked from the boards at which he pointed, to himself.

'True, sir. True. Precisely as it happened, so I tell it you.'

I could think of nothing to say, to any purpose, and my mouth was very dry. The wind and the wires took up the story with a long lamenting wail.

He resumed. 'Now, sir, mark this, and judge how my mind is troubled. The spectre came back, a week ago. Ever since, it has been there, now and again, by fits and starts.'

'At the light?'

'At the danger light.'

'What does it seem to do?'

He repeated, if possible with increased passion and vehemence, that former gesticulation of 'For God's sake clear the way!'

Then, he went on. 'I have no peace or rest for it. It calls to me, for many minutes together, in an agonised manner, "Below there! Look out! Look out!" It stands waving to me. It rings my little bell –'

I caught at that. 'Did it ring your bell yesterday evening when I was here, and you went to the door?'

'Twice.'

'Why, see,' said I, 'how your imagination misleads you. My eyes were on the bell, and my ears were open to the bell, and if I am a living man, it did NOT ring at those times. No, nor at any other time, except when it was rung in the natural course of physical things by the station communicating with you.'

He shook his head. 'I have never made a mistake as to that, yet, sir. I have never confused the spectre's ring with the man's. The ghost's ring is a strange vibration in the bell that it derives from nothing else, and I have not asserted that the bell stirs to the eye. I don't wonder that you failed to hear it. But *I* heard it.'

'And did the spectre seem to be there, when you looked out?'

'It *was* there.'

'Both times?'

He repeated firmly: 'Both times.'

'Will you come to the door with me, and look for it now?'

He bit his underlip as though he were somewhat unwilling, but arose. I opened the door and stood on the step, while he stood in the doorway. There, was the danger light. There, was the dismal mouth of the tunnel. There, were the high wet stone walls of the cutting. There, were the stars above them.

'Do you see it?' I asked him, taking particular note of his face. His eyes were prominent and strained; but not very much more so, perhaps, than my own had been when I had directed them earnestly towards the same spot.

'No,' he answered. 'It is not there.'

'Agreed,' said I.

We went in again, shut the door and resumed our seats. I was thinking how best to improve this advantage, if it might be called one, when he took up the conversation in such a matter of course way, so assuming that there could be no serious question of fact between us, that I felt myself placed in the weakest of positions.

'By this time you will fully understand, sir,' he said, 'that what troubles me so dreadfully is the question: What does the spectre mean?'

I was not sure, I told him, that I did fully understand.

'What is its warning against?' he said, ruminating, with his eyes on the fire, and only by times turning them on me. 'What is the danger? Where is the danger? There is danger overhanging, somewhere on the line. Some dreadful calamity will happen. It is not to be doubted this third time, after what has gone before. But surely this is a cruel haunting of *me*. What can *I* do?'

He pulled out his handkerchief and wiped the drops from his heated forehead.

'If I telegraph "danger", on either side of me, or on both, I can give no reason for it,' he went on, wiping the palms of his hands. 'I should get into trouble, and do no good. They would think I was mad. This is the way it would work – Message: "Danger! Take care!" Answer: "What danger? Where?" Message: "Don't know. But for God's sake take care!" They would displace me. What else could they do?'

His pain of mind was most pitiable to see. It was the mental torture of a conscientious man, oppressed beyond endurance by an unintelligible responsibility involving life.

'When it first stood under the danger light,' he went on, putting his dark hair back from his head, and drawing his hands outward across and across his temples in an extremity of feverish distress, 'why not tell me where that accident was to happen – if it must happen? Why not tell me how it could be averted – if it could have been averted? When on its

63

second coming it hid its face, why not tell me instead: "She is going to die. Let them keep her at home"? If it came, on those two occasions, only to show me that its warnings were true, and so to prepare me for the third, why not warn me plainly now? And I, Lord help me! A mere poor signalman on this solitary station! Why not go to somebody with credit to be believed, and power to act!'

When I saw him in this state, I saw that for the poor man's sake, as well as for the public safety, what I had to do for the time was to compose his mind. Therefore, setting aside all question of reality or unreality between us, I represented to him that whoever thoroughly discharged his duty must do well, and that at least it was his comfort that he understood his duty, though he did not understand these confounding appearances. In this effort I succeeded far better than in the attempt to reason him out of his conviction. He became calm; the occupations incidental to his post, as the night advanced, began to make larger demands on his attention, and I left him at two in the morning. I had offered to stay through the night, but he would not hear of it.

That I more than once looked back at the red light as I ascended the pathway – that I did not like the red light, and that I should have slept but poorly if my bed had been under it – I see no reason to conceal. Nor did I like the two sequences of the accident and the dead girl. I see no reason to conceal that, either.

But, what ran most in my thoughts was the consideration how ought I to act, having become the recipient of this disclosure? I had proved the man to be intelligent, vigilant, painstaking and exact; but how long might he remain so, in his state of mind? Though in a subordinate position, still he held a most important trust, and would I (for instance) like to stake my own life on the chances of his continuing to execute it with precision?

Unable to overcome a feeling that there would be something treacherous in my communicating what he had told me to his superiors in the company, without first being plain with himself and proposing a middle course to him, I ultimately resolved to offer to accompany him (otherwise keeping his secret for the present) to the wisest medical practitioner we could hear of in those parts, and to take his opinion. A change in his time of duty would come round next night, he had apprised me, and he would be off an hour or two after sunrise, and on again soon after sunset. I had appointed to return accordingly.

Next evening was a lovely evening, and I walked out early to enjoy it. The sun was not yet quite down when I traversed the field path near the top of the deep cutting. I would extend my walk for an hour, I said to myself, half an hour on and half an hour back, and it would then be time to go to my signalman's box.

Before pursuing my stroll, I stepped to the brink, and mechanically looked down, from the point from which I had first seen him. I cannot describe the thrill that seized upon me when, close at the mouth of the tunnel, I saw the appearance of a man, with his left sleeve across his eyes, passionately waving his right arm.

The nameless horror that oppressed me passed in a moment, for in a moment I saw that this appearance of a man was a man indeed, and that there was a little group of other men standing at a short distance, to whom he seemed to be rehearsing the gesture he made. The danger light was not yet lighted. Against its shaft, a little low hut, entirely new to me, had been made of some wooden supports and tarpaulin. It look-ed no bigger than a bed.

With an irresistible sense that something was wrong – with a flashing self-reproachful fear that fatal mischief had come of my leav-ing the man there, and causing no one to be sent to overlook or correct what he did – I descended the notched path with all the speed I could make.

'What is the matter?' I asked the men.

'Signalman killed this morning, sir.'

'Not the man belonging to that box?'

'Yes, sir.'

'Not the man I know?'

'You will recognise him, sir, if you knew him,' said the man who spoke for the others, solemnly uncovering his own head and raising an end of the tarpaulin, 'for his face is quite composed.'

'Oh! how did this happen, how did this happen?' I asked, turning from one to another as the hut closed in again.

'He was cut down by an engine, sir. No man in England knew his work better. But somehow he was not clear of the outer rail. It was just at broad day. He had struck the light, and had the lamp in his hand. As the engine came out of the tunnel, his back was towards her, and she cut him down. That man drove her, and was showing how it happened. Show the gentleman, Tom.'

The man, who wore a rough dark dress, stepped back to his former place at the mouth of the tunnel:

'Coming round the curve in the tunnel, sir,' he said, 'I saw him at the end, like as if I saw him down a perspective glass. There was no time to check speed, and I knew him to be very careful. As he didn't seem to take heed of the whistle, I shut it off when we were running down upon him, and called to him as loud as I could call.'

'What did you say?'

'I said, "Below there! Look out! Look out! For God's sake clear the way!"'

I started.

'Ah! it was a dreadful time, sir. I never left off calling to him. I put this arm before my eyes, not to see, and I waved this arm to the last – but it was no use.'

Without prolonging the narrative to dwell on any one of its curious circumstances more than on any other, I may, in closing it, point out the coincidence that the warning of the engine-driver included, not only the words which the unfortunate signalman had repeated to me as haunting him, but also the words which I myself – not he – had attached – and that only in my own mind – to the gesticulation he had imitated.

No. 2 BRANCH LINE. THE ENGINE-DRIVER
[by Andrew Halliday]

'Altogether? Well. Altogether, since 1841, I've killed seven men and boys. It ain't many in all those years.'

These startling words he uttered in a serious tone as he leant against the station wall. He was a thick-set, ruddy-faced man, with coal-black eyes, the whites of which were not white, but a brownish-yellow, and apparently scarred and seamed, as if they had been operated upon. They were eyes that had worked hard in looking through wind and weather. He was dressed in a short black pea-jacket and grimy white canvas trousers, and wore on his head a flat black cap. There was no sign of levity in his face. His look was serious even to sadness, and there was an air of responsibility about his whole bearing which assured me that he spoke in earnest.

'Yes, sir, I have been for five-and-twenty years a locomotive engine-driver; and in all that time, I've only killed seven men and boys. There's not many of my mates as can say as much for themselves. Steadiness, sir – steadiness and keeping your eyes open, is what does it. When I say seven men and boys, I mean my mates – stokers, porters, and so forth. I don't count passengers.'

How did he become an engine-driver?

'My father,' he said, 'was a wheelwright in a small way, and lived in a little cottage by the side of the railway which runs betwixt Leeds and Selby. It was the second railway laid down in the kingdom, the second after the Liverpool and Manchester, where Mr Huskisson was killed, as you may have heard on, sir. When the trains rushed by, we young 'uns used to run out to look at 'em, and hurray. I noticed the driver turning handles, and making it go, and I thought to myself it would be a fine thing to be a engine-driver, and have the control of a wonderful machine like that. Before the railway, the driver of the mail coach was the biggest man I knew. I thought I should like to be the driver of a coach. We had a picture in our cottage of George the third in a red coat. I always mixed up the driver of the mail coach – who had a red coat, too – with the King, only he had a low-crowned broad-brimmed hat, which the King hadn't. In my idea, the King couldn't be a greater man than the driver of the mail coach. I had always a fancy to be head man of some kind. When I went to Leeds once, and saw a man conducting a orchestra, I thought I should like to be the conductor of a orchestra. When I went home I made myself a baton, and went about the fields conducting a orchestra. It wasn't there, of course, but I pretended it was. At another time, a man with a whip and a speaking trumpet, on the stage outside a show, took my fancy, and I thought I should like to be him. But when the train came, the engine-driver put them all in the shade, and I was resolved to be a engine-driver. It wasn't long before I had to do something to earn my own living, though I was only a young 'un. My father died suddenly – he was killed by thunder and lightning while standing under a tree out of the rain – and mother couldn't keep us all. The day after my father's burial I walked down to the station, and said I wanted to be a engine-driver. The stationmaster laughed a bit, said I was for beginning early, but that I was not quite big enough yet. He gave me a penny, and told me to go home and grow, and come again in ten years' time. I didn't dream of danger then. If I couldn't be a engine-driver, I was determined to have something to do about a engine; so, as I could get nothing else, I went on board a Humber steamer, and broke up coals for the stoker. That was how I began. From that, I became a stoker, first on board a boat, and then on a locomotive. Then, after two years' service, I became a driver on the very line which passed our cottage. My mother and my brothers and sisters came out to look at me, the first day I drove. I was watching for them and they was watching for me, and they waved their hands and hurrayed, and I waved my hand to them. I had the steam well up, and was going at a rattling pace, and rare proud I was that minute. Never was so proud in my life!

'When a man has a liking for a thing it's as good as being clever. In a very short time I became one of the best drivers on the line. That was allowed. I took a pride in it, you see, and liked it. No, I didn't know much about the engine scientifically, as you call it; but I could put her to rights if anything went out of gear – that is to say, if there was nothing broken – but I couldn't have explained how the steam worked inside. Starting a engine is just like drawing a drop of gin. You turn a handle and off she goes; then you turn the handle the other way, put on the brakes, and you stop her. There's not much more in it, so far. It's no good being scientific and knowing the principle of the engine inside – no good at all. Fitters, who know all the ins and outs of the engine, make the worst drivers. That's well known. They know too much. It's just as I've heard of a man with regard to *his* inside: if he knew what a complicated machine it is, he would never eat, or drink, or dance, or run, or do anything, for fear of busting something. So it is with fitters. But us as are not troubled with such thoughts, *we* go ahead.

'But starting a engine's one thing and driving of her is another. Anyone, a child a'most, can turn on the steam and turn it off again; but it ain't everyone that can keep a engine well on the road, no more than it ain't everyone who can ride a horse properly. It is much the same thing. If you gallop a horse right off for a mile or two, you take the wind out of him, and for the next mile or two you must let him trot or walk. So it is with a engine. If you put on too much steam, to get over the ground at the start, you exhaust the boiler, and then you'll have to crawl along till your fresh water boils up. The great thing in driving is to go steady, never to let your water get too low, nor your fire too low. It's the same with a kettle. If you fill it up when it's about half empty, it soon comes to the boil again; but if you don't fill it up until the water's nearly out, it's a long time in coming to the boil again. Another thing; you should never make spurts, unless you are detained and lose time. You should go up a incline and down a incline at the same pace. Sometimes a driver will waste his steam, and when he comes to a hill he has scarcely enough to drag him up. When you're in a train that goes by fits and starts, you may be sure that there is a bad driver on the engine. That kind of driving frightens passengers dreadful. When the train, after rattling along, suddenly slackens speed when it ain't near a station, it may be in the middle of a tunnel, the passengers think there is danger. But generally it's because the driver has exhausted his steam.

'I drove the Brighton express, four or five years before I come here, and the annuals – that is, the passengers who had annual tickets – always said they knew when I was on the engine, because they wasn't jerked. Gentlemen used to say as they came onto the platform, "Who drives today – Jim Martin?" And when the guard told them yes, they said, "All right," and took their seats quite comfortable. But the driver never gets so much as a shilling; the guard comes in for all that, and he does nothing much. Few ever think of the driver. I dare say they think the train goes along of itself; yet if we didn't keep a sharp lookout, know our duty, and do it, they might all go smash at any moment. I used to make that journey to Brighton in fifty-two minutes. The papers said forty-nine minutes, but that was coming it a little too strong. I had to watch signals all the way, one every two miles, so that me and my stoker were on the stretch all the time, doing two things at once – attending to the engine and looking out. I've driven on this line, eighty-one miles and three-quarters, in eighty-six minutes. There's no danger in speed if you have a good road, a good engine, and not too many coaches behind. No, we don't call them carriages, we call them "coaches".

'Yes, oscillation means danger. If you're ever in a coach that oscillates much, tell of it at the first station and get it coupled up closer. Coaches when they're too loose are apt to jump, or swing off the rails; and it's quite as dangerous when they're coupled up too close. There ought to be just space enough for the buffers to work easy. Passengers are frightened in tunnels, but there's less danger, *now*, in tunnels than anywhere else. We never enter a tunnel unless it's signalled clear.

'A train can be stopped wonderful quick, even when running express, if the guards act with the driver and clap on all the brakes promptly. Much depends upon the guards. One brake behind is as good as two in front. The engine, you see, loses weight as she burns her coals and consumes her water, but the coaches behind don't alter. We have a good deal of trouble with young guards. In their anxiety to perform their duties, they put on the brakes too soon, so that sometimes we can scarcely drag the train into the station; when they grow older at it they are not so anxious, and don't put them on soon enough. It's no use to say, when an accident happens, that they did not put on the brakes in time; they swear they did, and you can't prove that they didn't.

'Do I think that the tapping of the wheels with a hammer is a mere ceremony? Well, I don't know exactly; I should not like to say. It's not often that the chaps find anything wrong. They may sometimes be half asleep when a train comes into a station in the middle of the night. You would be yourself. They ought to tap the axle box, but they don't.

'Many accidents take place that never get into the papers; many trains, full of passengers, escape being dashed to pieces next door to a miracle. Nobody knows anything about it but the driver and the stoker. I remember once, when I was driving on the Eastern Counties. Going round a curve, I suddenly saw a train coming along on the same line of rails. I clapped on the brake, but it was too late, I thought. Seeing the engine almost close upon us, I cried to my stoker to jump. He jumped off the engine, almost before the words were out of my mouth. I was just taking my hand off the lever to follow, when the coming train turned off on the points, and the next instant the hind coach passed my engine by a shave. It was the nearest touch I ever saw. My stoker was killed. In another half-second I should have jumped off and been killed too. What would have become of the train without us is more than I can tell you.

'There are heaps of people run over that no one ever hears about. One dark night in the Black Country, me and my mate felt something wet and warm splash in our faces. "That didn't come from the engine, Bill," I said. "No," he said; "it's something thick, Jim." It was blood. That's what it was. We heard afterwards that a collier had been run over. When we kill any of our own chaps, we say as little about it as possible. It's generally – mostly always – their own fault. No, we never think of danger ourselves. We're used to it, you see. But we're not reckless. I don't believe there's any body of men that takes more pride in their own work than engine-drivers do. We are as proud and as fond of our engines as if they were living things; as proud of them as a huntsman or a jockey is of his horse. And a engine has almost as many ways as a horse – she's a kicker, a plunger, a roarer, or what not, in her way. Put a stranger onto my engine, and he wouldn't know what to do with her. Yes, there's wonderful improvements in engines since the last Great Exhibition.[3] Some of them take up their water without stopping. That's a wonderful invention, and yet as simple as ABC. There are water troughs at certain places, lying between the rails. By moving a lever you let down the mouth of a scoop into the water, and as you rush along the water is forced into the tank, at the rate of three thousand gallons a minute.

'A engine-driver's chief anxiety is to keep time – that's what he thinks most of. When I was driving the Brighton express, I always felt like as if

I was riding a race against time. I had no fear of the pace; what I feared was losing way, and not getting in to the minute. We have to give in an account of our time when we arrive. The company provides us with watches, and we go by them. Before starting on a journey, we pass through a room to be inspected. That's to see if we are sober. But they don't say nothing to us, and a man who was a little gone might pass easy. I've known a stoker that had passed the inspection, come on to the engine as drunk as a fly, flop down among the coals, and sleep there like a log for the whole run. I had to be my own stoker then. If you ask me if engine-drivers are drinking men, I must answer you that they are pretty well. It's trying work: one half of you cold as ice, t'other half hot as fire – wet one minute, dry the next. If ever a man had an excuse for drinking, that man's a engine-driver. And yet I don't know if ever a driver goes upon his engine drunk. If he was to, the wind would soon sober him.

'I believe engine-drivers, as a body, are the healthiest fellows alive; but they don't live long. The cause of that I believe to be the cold food and the shaking. By the cold food I mean that a engine-driver never gets his meals comfortable. He's never at home to his dinner. When he starts away the first thing in the morning, he takes a bit of cold meat and a piece of bread with him for his dinner; and generally he has to eat it in the shed, for he mustn't leave his engine. You can understand how the jolting and shaking knocks a man up, after a bit. The insurance companies won't take us at ordinary rates. We're obliged to be Foresters, or Old Friends,[4] or that sort of thing, where they ain't so particular. The wages of a engine-driver average about eight shillings a day, but if he's a good schemer with his coals – yes, I mean if he economises his coals – he's allowed so much more. Some will make from five to ten shillings a week that way. I don't complain of the wages particular, but it's hard lines for such as us, to have to pay income tax. The company gives an account of all our wages, and we have to pay. It's a shame.

'Our domestic life – our life at home, you mean? Well, as to that, we don't see much of our families. I leave home at half-past seven in the morning, and don't get back again until half-past nine, or maybe later. The children are not up when I leave, and they've gone to bed again before I come home. This is about my day: leave London at 8.45, drive for four hours and a half, cold snack on the engine step, see to engine, drive back again, clean engine, report myself, and home. Twelve hours' hard and anxious work, and no comfortable victuals. Yes, our wives are anxious about us, for we never know, when we go out, if we'll ever come back again. We ought to go home the minute we leave the station, and report ourselves to those that are thinking on us and depending on us; but I'm afraid we don't always. Perhaps we go first to the public house, and perhaps you would, too, if you were in charge of a engine all day long. But the wives have a way of their own of finding out if we're all right. They enquire among each other. "Have you seen my Jim?" one says. "No," says another, "but Jack see him coming out of the station half an hour ago." Then she knows that her Jim's all right, and knows where to find him if she wants him. It's a sad thing when any of us have to carry bad news to a mate's wife. None of us likes that job. I remember, when Jack Davidge was killed, none of us could face his poor missus with the news. She had seven children, poor thing, and two of 'em, the youngest, was down with the fever. We got old Mrs Berridge – Tom Berridge's mother – to break it to her. But she knew summat was the matter the minute the old woman went in, and, afore she spoke a word, fell down like as if she was dead. She lay all night like that, and never heard from mortal lips until next morning that her Jack was killed. But she knew it in her heart. It's a pitch and toss kind of a life ours!

'And yet I never was nervous on a engine but once. I never think of my own life. You go in for staking that, when you begin, and you get used to the risk. I never think of the passengers either. The thoughts of a engine-driver never go behind his engine. If he keeps his engine all right, the coaches behind will be all right, as far as the driver is concerned. But once I *did* think of the passengers. My little boy, Bill, was among them that morning. He was a poor little cripple fellow that we all loved more nor the others, because he *was* a cripple, and so quiet and wise-like. He was going down to his aunt in the country, who was to take care of him for a while. We thought the country air would do him good. I did think there were lives behind me that morning; at least, I thought hard of one little life that was in my hands. There were twenty coaches on; my little Bill seemed to me to be in every one of 'em. My hand trembled as I turned on the steam. I felt my heart thumping as we drew close to the pointsman's box; as we neared the Junction, I was all in a cold sweat. At the end of the first fifty miles I was nearly eleven minutes behind time. "What's the matter with you this morning?" my stoker said. "Did you have a drop too much last night?" "Don't speak to me, Fred," I said, "till we get to Peterborough; and keep a sharp lookout, there's a good fellow." I never was so thankful in my life as when I shut off steam to enter the station at Peterborough. Little Bill's aunt was waiting for him, and I saw her lift him out of the carriage. I called out to her to bring him to me, and I took him upon the engine and kissed him – ah, twenty times I should think – making him in such a mess with grease and coal dust as you never saw.

'I was all right for the rest of the journey. And I do believe, sir, the passengers were safer after little Bill was gone. It would never do, you see, for engine-drivers to know too much, or to feel too much.'

No. 3 BRANCH LINE. THE COMPENSATION HOUSE

[by Charles Collins]

'There's not a looking glass in all the house, sir. It's some peculiar fancy of my master's. There isn't one in any single room in the house.'

It was a dark and gloomy-looking building, and had been purchased by this company for an enlargement of their goods station. The value of the house had been referred to what was popularly called 'a compensation jury', and the house was called, in consequence, 'the compensation house'. It had become the company's property; but its tenant still remained in possession, pending the commencement of active building operations. My attention was originally drawn to this house because it stood directly in front of a collection of huge pieces of timber which lay near this part of the line, and on which I sometimes sat for half an hour at a time, when I was tired by my wanderings about Mugby Junction.

It was square, cold, grey-looking, built of rough-hewn stone, and roofed with thin slabs of the same material. Its windows were few in number, and very small for the size of the building. In the great, blank, grey broadside there were only four windows. The entrance door was in the middle of the house; there was a window on either side of it, and there were two more in the single storey above. The blinds were all closely drawn and, when the door was shut, the dreary building gave no sign of life or occupation.

But the door was not always shut. Sometimes it was opened from within, with a great jingling of bolts and door chains, and then a man would come forward and stand upon the doorstep, snuffing the air as one might do who was ordinarily kept on rather a small allowance of that element. He was stout, thickset, and perhaps fifty or sixty years old – a man whose hair was cut exceedingly close, who wore a large bushy beard, and whose eye had a sociable twinkle in it which was prepossessing. He was dressed, whenever I saw him, in a greenish-brown frock coat made of some material which was not cloth, wore a waistcoat and trousers of light colour, and had a frill to his shirt – an ornament, by the way, which did not seem to go at all well with the beard, which was continually in contact with it. It was the custom of this worthy person, after standing for a short time on the threshold inhaling the air, to come forward into the road and, after glancing at one of the upper windows in a half-mechanical way, to cross over to the logs and, leaning over the fence which guarded the railway, to look up and down the line (it passed before the house) with the air of a man accomplishing a self-imposed task of which nothing was expected to come. This done, he would cross the road again, and turning on the threshold to take a final sniff of air, disappeared once more within the house, bolting and chaining the door again as if there were no probability of its being reopened for at least a week. Yet half an hour had not passed before he was out in the road again, sniffing the air and looking up and down the line as before.

It was not very long before I managed to scrape acquaintance with this restless personage. I soon found out that my friend with the shirt-frill was the confidential servant, butler, valet, factotum, what you will, of a sick gentleman, a Mr Oswald Strange, who had recently come to inhabit the house opposite, and concerning whose history my new acquaintance, whose name I ascertained was Masey, seemed disposed to be somewhat communicative. His master, it appeared, had come down to this place partly for the sake of reducing his establishment – not, Mr Masey was swift to inform me, on economical principles, but because the poor gentleman, for particular reasons, wished to have few dependents about him – partly in order that he might be near his old friend, Dr Garden, who was established in the neighbourhood, and whose society and advice were necessary to Mr Strange's life. That life was, it appeared, held by this suffering gentleman on a precarious tenure. It was ebbing away fast with each passing hour. The servant already spoke of his master in the past tense, describing him to me as a young gentleman not more than five-and-thirty years of age, with a young face, as far as the features and build of it went, but with an expression which had nothing of youth about it. This was the great peculiarity of the man. At a distance he looked younger than he was by many years, and strangers, at the time when he had been used to get about, always took him for a man of seven or eight-and-twenty, but they changed their minds on getting nearer to him. Old Masey had a way of his own of summing up the peculiarities of his master, repeating twenty times over: 'Sir, he was Strange by name and Strange by nature, and Strange to look at into the bargain.'

It was during my second or third interview with the old fellow that he uttered the words quoted at the beginning of this plain narrative.

'Not such a thing as a looking glass in all the house,' the old man said, standing beside my piece of timber, and looking across reflectively at the house opposite. 'Not one.'

'In the sitting rooms, I suppose you mean?'

'No, sir, I mean sitting rooms and bedrooms both; there isn't so much as a shaving glass as big as the palm of your hand anywhere.'

'But how is it?' I asked. 'Why are there no looking glasses in any of the rooms?'

'Ah, sir!' replied Masey, 'that's what none of us can ever tell. There is the mystery. It's just a fancy on the part of my master. He had some strange fancies, and this was one of them. A pleasant gentleman he was to live with, as any servant could desire. A liberal gentleman, and one who gave but little trouble; always ready with a kind word, and a kind deed, too, for the matter of that. There was not a house in all the parish of St George's (in which we lived before we came down here) where the servants had more holidays or a better table kept; but, for all that, he had his queer ways and his fancies, as I may call them, and this was one of them. And the point he made of it, sir,' the old man went on, 'the extent to which that regulation was enforced, whenever a new servant was engaged, and the changes in the establishment it occasioned! In hiring a new servant, the very first stipulation made was that about the looking glasses. It was one of my duties to explain the thing, as far as it could be explained, before any servant was taken into the house. "You'll find it an easy place," I used to say, "with a liberal table, good wages, and a deal of leisure; but there's one thing you must make up your mind to: you must do without looking glasses while you're here, for there isn't one in the house and, what's more, there never will be."'

'But how did you know there never would be one?' I asked.

'Lor' bless you, sir! If you'd seen and heard all that I'd seen and heard, you could have no doubt about it. Why, only to take one instance – I remember a particular day when my master had occasion to go into the housekeeper's room, where the cook lived, to see about some alterations that were making, and when a pretty scene took place. The cook – she was a very ugly woman, and awful vain – had left a little bit of a looking glass, about six inches square, upon the chimney piece; she had got it *surreptious*, and kept it always locked up; but she'd left it out, being called away suddenly, while titivating her hair. I had seen the glass, and was making for the chimney piece as fast as I could, but master came in front of it before I could get there, and it was all over in a moment. He gave one long piercing look into it, turned deadly pale and, seizing the glass, dashed it into a hundred pieces on the floor, and then stamped upon the fragments and ground them into powder with his feet. He shut himself up for the rest of that day in his own room, first ordering me to discharge the cook, then and there, at a moment's notice.'

'What an extraordinary thing!' I said, pondering.

'Ah, sir,' continued the old man, 'it was astonishing what trouble I had with those women-servants. It was difficult to get any that would take the place at all under the circumstances. "What, not so much as a mossul to do one's 'air at?" they would say, and they'd go off, in spite of extra wages. Then those who did consent to come, what lies they would tell, to be sure! They would protest that they didn't want to look in the glass, that they never had been in the habit of looking in the glass, and all the while that very wench would have her looking glass, of some kind or another, hid away among her clothes upstairs. Sooner or later, she would bring it out too, and leave it about somewhere or other (just like the cook), where it was as likely as not that master might see it. And then – for girls like that have no consciences, sir – when I had caught one of 'em at it, she'd turn round as bold as brass, "And how am I to know whether my 'air's parted straight?" she'd say, just as if it hadn't been considered in her wages that that was the very thing which she never *was* to know while she lived in our house. A vain lot, sir, and the ugly ones always the vainest. There was no end to their dodges. They'd have looking glasses in the interiors of their workbox lids, where it was next to impossible that I could find 'em, or inside the covers of hymn books, or cookery books, or in their caddies. I recollect one girl, a sly one she was, and marked with the smallpox terrible, who was always reading her Prayer Book at odd times. Sometimes I used to think what a religious mind she'd got, and at other times (depending on the mood I was in) I would conclude that it was the marriage service she was studying; but one day, when I got behind her to satisfy my doubts – lo and behold! – it was the old story: a bit of glass, without a frame, fastened into the kiver with the outside edges of the sheets of postage stamps. Dodges! Why, they'd keep their looking glasses in the scullery or the coal-cellar, or leave them in charge of the servants next door, or with the milkwoman round the corner – but have 'em they would. And I don't mind confessing, sir,' said the old man, bringing his long speech to an end, 'that it *was* an inconveniency not to have so much as a scrap to shave before. I used to go to the barber's at first, but I soon gave that up, and took to wearing my beard as my master did; likewise to keeping my hair' – Mr Masey touched his head as he spoke – 'so short that it didn't require any parting, before or behind.'

I sat for some time lost in amazement, and staring at my companion. My curiosity was powerfully stimulated, and the desire to learn more was very strong within me.

'Had your master any personal defect,' I enquired, 'which might have made it distressing to him to see his own image reflected?'

'By no means, sir,' said the old man. 'He was as handsome a gentleman as you would wish to see: a little delicate-looking and careworn – perhaps, with a very pale face, but as free from any deformity as you or I, sir. No, sir, no; it was nothing of that.'

'Then what was it? What is it?' I asked, desperately. 'Is there no one who is, or has been, in your master's confidence?'

'Yes, sir,' said the old fellow, with his eyes turning to that window opposite. 'There is one person who knows all my master's secrets, and this secret among the rest.'

'And who is that?'

The old man turned round and looked at me fixedly. 'The doctor here,' he said. 'Dr Garden. My master's very old friend.'

'I should like to speak with this gentleman,' I said, involuntarily.

'He is with my master now,' answered Masey. 'He will be coming out presently, and I think I may say he will answer any question you may like to put to him.' As the old man spoke, the door of the house opened, and a middle-aged gentleman, who was tall and thin, but who lost something of his height by a habit of stooping, appeared on the step. Old Masey left me in a moment. He muttered something about taking the doctor's directions, and hastened across the road. The tall gentleman spoke to him for a minute or two very seriously, probably about the patient upstairs, and it then seemed to me from their gestures that I myself was the subject of some further conversation between them. At all events, when old Masey retired into the house, the doctor came across to where I was standing, and addressed me with a very agreeable smile.

'John Masey tells me that you are interested in the case of my poor friend, sir. I am now going back to my house, and if you don't mind the trouble of walking with me, I shall be happy to enlighten you as far as I am able.'

I hastened to make my apologies and express my acknowledgements, and we set off together. When we had reached the doctor's house and were seated in his study, I ventured to enquire after the health of this poor gentleman.

'I am afraid there is no amendment, nor any prospect of amendment,' said the doctor. 'Old Masey has told you something of his strange condition, has he not?'

'Yes, he has told me something,' I answered, 'and he says you know all about it.'

Dr Garden looked very grave. 'I don't know all about it. I only know what happens when he comes into the presence of a looking glass. But as to the circumstances which have led to his being haunted in the strangest fashion that I ever heard of, I know no more of them than you do.'

'Haunted?' I repeated. 'And in the strangest fashion that you ever heard of?'

Dr Garden smiled at my eagerness, seemed to be collecting his thoughts, and presently went on:

'I made the acquaintance of Mr Oswald Strange in a curious way. It was on board of an Italian steamer, bound from Civitavecchia to Marseilles. We had been travelling all night. In the morning I was shaving myself in the cabin, when suddenly this man came behind me, glanced for a moment into the small mirror before which I was standing, and then, without a word of warning, tore it from the nail, and dashed it to pieces at my feet. His face was at first livid with passion – it seemed to me rather the passion of fear than of anger – but it changed after a moment, and he seemed ashamed of what he had done. Well,' continued the doctor, relapsing for a moment into a smile, 'of course I was in a devil of a rage. I was operating on my underjaw, and the start the thing gave me caused me to cut myself. Besides, altogether it seemed an outrageous and insolent thing, and I gave it to poor Strange in a style of language which I am sorry to think of now, but which, I hope, was excusable at the time. As to the offender himself, his confusion and regret, now that his passion was at an end, disarmed me. He sent for the steward, and paid most liberally for the damage done to the steamboat property, explaining to him, and to some other passengers who were present in the cabin, that what had happened had been accidental. For me, however, he had another explanation. Perhaps he felt that I must know it to have been no accident – perhaps he really wished to confide in someone. At all events, he owned to me that what he had done was done under the influence of an uncontrollable impulse – a seizure which took him, he said, at times – something like a fit. He begged my pardon, and entreated that I would endeavour to disassociate him personally from this action, of which he was heartily ashamed. Then he attempted a sickly joke, poor fellow, about his wearing a beard, and feeling a little spiteful, in consequence, when he saw other people taking the trouble to shave; but he said nothing about any infirmity or delusion, and shortly after left me.

'In my professional capacity I could not help taking some interest in Mr Strange. I did not altogether lose sight of him after our sea journey to Marseilles was over. I found him a pleasant companion up to a certain point; but I always felt that there was a reserve about him. He was uncommunicative about his past life, and especially would never allude to anything connected with his travels or his residence in Italy, which, however, I could make out had been a long one. He spoke Italian well, and seemed familiar with the country, but disliked to talk about it.

'During the time we spent together there were seasons when he was so little himself that I, with a pretty large experience, was almost afraid to be with him. His attacks were violent and sudden in the last degree;

and there was one most extraordinary feature connected with them all: some horrible association of ideas took possession of him whenever he found himself before a looking glass. And after we had travelled together for a time, I dreaded the sight of a mirror hanging harmlessly against a wall, or a toilet-glass standing on a dressing table, almost as much as he did.

'Poor Strange was not always affected in the same manner by a looking glass. Sometimes it seemed to madden him with fury; at other times, it appeared to turn him to stone: remaining motionless and speechless as if attacked by catalepsy. One night – the worst things always happen at night, and oftener than one would think on stormy nights – we arrived at a small town in the central district of Auvergne: a place but little known, out of the line of railways, and to which we had been drawn partly by the antiquarian attractions which the place possessed, and partly by the beauty of the scenery. The weather had been rather against us. The day had been dull and murky, the heat stifling, and the sky had threatened mischief since the morning. At sundown, these threats were fulfilled. The thunderstorm, which had been all day coming up – as it seemed to us, against the wind – burst over the place where we were lodged, with very great violence.

'There are some practical-minded persons with strong constitutions, who deny roundly that their fellow creatures are, or can be, affected, in mind and body, by atmospheric influences. I am not a disciple of that school, simply because I cannot believe that those changes of weather, which have so much effect upon animals, and even on inanimate objects, can fail to have some influence on a piece of machinery so sensitive and intricate as the human frame. I think, then, that it was in part owing to the disturbed state of the atmosphere that, on this particular evening, I felt nervous and depressed. When my new friend Strange and I parted for the night, I felt as little disposed to go to rest as I ever did in my life. The thunder was still lingering among the mountains in the midst of which our inn was placed. Sometimes it seemed nearer, and at other times further off; but it never left off altogether, except for a few minutes at a time. It was quite unable to shake off a succession of painful ideas which persistently besieged my mind.

'It is hardly necessary to add that I thought from time to time of my travelling companion in the next room. His image was almost continually before me. He had been dull and depressed all the evening, and when we parted for the night there was a look in his eyes which I could not get out of my memory.

'There was a door between our rooms, and the partition dividing them was not very solid; and yet I had heard no sound since I parted from him which could indicate that he was there at all, much less that he was awake and stirring. I was in a mood, sir, which made this silence terrible to me, and so many foolish fancies – as that he was lying there dead, or in a fit, or what not – took possession of me, that at last I could bear it no longer. I went to the door and, after listening, very attentively but quite in vain, for any sound, I at last knocked pretty sharply. There was no answer. Feeling that longer suspense would be unendurable, I, without more ceremony, turned the handle and went in.

'It was a great bare room, and so imperfectly lighted by a single candle that it was almost impossible – except when the lightning flashed – to see into its great dark corners. A small rickety bedstead stood against one of the walls, shrouded by yellow cotton curtains passed through a great iron ring in the ceiling. There was, for all other furniture, an old chest of drawers which served also as a washing-stand, having a small basin and ewer and a single towel arranged on the top of it. There were, moreover, two ancient chairs and a dressing-table. On this last, stood a large old-fashioned looking glass with a carved frame.

'I must have seen all these things, because I remember them so well now, but I do not know how I could have seen them, for it seems to me that, from the moment of my entering that room, the action of my senses and of the faculties of my mind was held fast by the ghastly figure which stood motionless before the looking glass in the middle of the empty room.

'How terrible it was! The weak light of one candle standing on the table shone upon Strange's face, lighting it from below, and throwing (as I now remember) his shadow, vast and black, upon the wall behind him and upon the ceiling overhead. He was leaning rather forward, with his hands upon the table supporting him, and gazing into the glass

83

which stood before him with a horrible fixity. The sweat was on his white face; his rigid features and his pale lips shown in that feeble light were horrible, more than words can tell, to look at. He was so completely stupified and lost that the noise I had made in knocking and in entering the room was unobserved by him. Not even when I called him loudly by name did he move or did his face change.

'What a vision of horror that was, in the great dark empty room, in a silence that was something more than negative, that ghastly figure frozen into stone by some unexplained terror! And the silence and the stillness! The very thunder had ceased now. My heart stood still with fear. Then, moved by some instinctive feeling, under whose influence I acted mechanically, I crept with slow steps nearer and nearer to the table, and at last, half expecting to see some spectre even more horrible than this which I saw already, I looked over his shoulder into the looking glass. I happened to touch his arm, though only in the lightest manner. In that one moment the spell which had held him – who knows how long? – enchained, seemed broken, and he lived in this world again. He turned round upon me, as suddenly as a tiger makes its spring, and seized me by the arm.

'I have told you that even before I entered my friend's room I had felt, all that night, depressed and nervous. The necessity for action at this time was, however, so obvious, and this man's agony made all that I had felt appear so trifling, that much of my own discomfort seemed to leave me. I felt that I *must* be strong.

'The face before me almost unmanned me. The eyes which looked into mine were so scared with terror, the lips – if I may say so – looked so speechless. The wretched man gazed long into my face, and then, still holding me by the arm, slowly, very slowly, turned his head. I had gently tried to move him away from the looking glass, but he would not stir, and now he was looking into it as fixedly as ever. I could bear this no longer and, using such force as was necessary, I drew him gradually away, and got him to one of the chairs at the foot of the bed. "Come!" I said – after the long silence my voice, even to myself, sounded strange and hollow – "come! You are overtired, and you feel the weather. Don't you think you ought to be in bed? Suppose you lie down. Let me try my medical skill in mixing you a composing draught."

'He held my hand, and looked eagerly into my eyes. "I am better now," he said speaking at last very faintly. Still he looked at me in that wistful way. It seemed as if there were something that he wanted to do or say, but had not sufficient resolution. At length he got up from the chair to which I had led him, and beckoning me to follow him, went across the room to the dressing table, and stood again before the glass. A violent shudder passed through his frame as he looked into it; but, apparently forcing himself to go through with what he had now begun, he remained where he was and, without looking away, moved to me with his hand to come and stand beside him. I complied.

'"Look in there!" he said, in an almost inaudible tone. He was supported, as before, by his hands resting on the table, and could only bow with his head towards the glass to intimate what he meant. "Look in there!" he repeated.

'I did as he asked me.

'"What do you see?" he asked next.

'"See?" I repeated, trying to speak as cheerfully as I could, and describing the reflection of his own face as nearly as I could. "I see a very, very pale face with sunken cheeks –"

'"What?" he cried, with an alarm in his voice which I could not understand.

'"With sunken cheeks," I went on, "and two hollow eyes with large pupils."

'I saw the reflection of my friend's face change, and felt his hand clutch my arm even more tightly than he had done before. I stopped abruptly and looked round at him. He did not turn his head towards me, but, gazing still into the looking glass, seemed to labour for utterance.

'"What," he stammered at last. "Do – you – see – it – too?"

'"See what?" I asked, quickly.

'"That face!" he cried, in accents of horror. "That face – which is not mine – and which – I SEE INSTEAD OF MINE – always!"

'I was struck speechless by the words. In a moment this mystery was explained – but what an explanation! Worse, a hundred times worse, than anything I had imagined. What! Had this man lost the power of seeing his own image as it was reflected there before him? And, in its place, was there the image of another? Had he changed reflections with some other man? The frightfulness of the thought struck me speechless for a time – then I saw how false an impression my silence was conveying.

' "No, no, no!" I cried, as soon as I could speak – "a hundred times, no! I see you, of course, and only you. It was your face I attempted to describe, and no other."

'He seemed not to hear me. "Why, look there!" he said, in a low, indistinct voice, pointing to his own image in the glass. "Whose face do you see there?"

' "Why, yours, of course." And then, after a moment I added, "Whose do you see?"

'He answered, like one in a trance, "*His* – only his – always his!" He stood still a moment, and then, with a loud and terrific scream, repeated those words, "ALWAYS HIS, ALWAYS HIS", and fell down in a fit before me.'

'I knew what to do now. Here was a thing which, at any rate, I could understand. I had with me my usual small stock of medicines and surgical instruments, and I did what was necessary: first to restore my unhappy patient, and next to procure for him the rest he needed so much. He was very ill – at death's door for some days – and I could not leave him, though there was urgent need that I should be back in London. When he began to mend, I sent over to England for my servant – John Masey – whom I knew I could trust. Acquainting him with the outlines of the case, I left him in charge of my patient, with orders that he should be brought over to this country as soon as he was fit to travel.

'That awful scene was always before me. I saw this devoted man day after day, with the eyes of my imagination, sometimes destroying in his rage the harmless looking glass which was the immediate cause of his suffering, sometimes transfixed before the horrid image that turned him to stone. I recollect coming upon him once when we were stopping at a roadside inn, and seeing him stand so by broad daylight. His back was turned towards me, and I waited and watched him for nearly half an hour as he stood there motionless and speechless, and appearing not to breathe. I am not sure but that this apparition seen so by daylight was more ghastly than that apparition seen in the middle of the night, with the thunder rumbling among the hills.

'Back in London in his own house, where he could command in some sort the objects which should surround him, poor Strange was better than he would have been elsewhere. He seldom went out except at night, but once or twice I have walked with him by daylight, and have seen him terribly agitated when we have had to pass a shop in which looking glasses were exposed for sale.

'It is nearly a year now since my poor friend followed me down to this place, to which I have retired. For some months he has been daily getting weaker and weaker, and a disease of the lungs has become developed in him, which has brought him to his deathbed. I should add, by the by, that John Masey has been his constant companion ever since I brought them together, and I have had, consequently, to look after a new servant.

'And now tell me,' the doctor added, bringing his tale to an end, 'did you ever hear a more miserable history, or was ever man haunted in a more ghastly manner than this man?'

I was about to reply, when we heard a sound of footsteps outside and, before I could speak, old Masey entered the room, in haste and disorder.

'I was just telling this gentleman,' the doctor said – not at the moment observing old Masey's changed manner – 'how you deserted me to go over to your present master.'

'Ah! sir,' the man answered, in a troubled voice, 'I'm afraid he won't be my master long.'

The doctor was on his legs in a moment. 'What! Is he worse?'

'I think, sir, he is dying,' said the old man.

'Come with me, sir; you may be of use if you can keep quiet.' The doctor caught up his hat as he addressed me in those words, and in a few minutes we had reached the compensation house. A few seconds more and we were standing in a darkened room on the first floor, and I saw lying on a bed before me – pale, emaciated and, as it seemed, dying – the man whose story I had just heard.

He was lying with closed eyes when we came into the room, and I had leisure to examine his features.

What a tale of misery they told! They were regular and symmetrical in their arrangement, and not without beauty – the beauty of exceeding refinement and delicacy. Force there was none, and perhaps it was to the want of this that the faults – perhaps the crime – which had made the man's life so miserable were to be attributed. Perhaps the crime? Yes, it was not likely that an affliction, lifelong and terrible, such as this he had endured would come upon him, unless some misdeed had provoked the punishment. What misdeed we were soon to know.

It sometimes – I think generally – happens that the presence of anyone who stands and watches beside a sleeping man will wake him, unless his slumbers are unusually heavy. It was so now. While we looked at him, the sleeper awoke very suddenly, and fixed his eyes upon us. He put out his hand and took the doctor's in its feeble grasp. 'Who is that?' he asked next, pointing towards me.

'Do you wish him to go? The gentleman knows something of your sufferings, and is powerfully interested in your case; but he will leave us, if you wish it,' the doctor said.

'No. Let him stay.'

Seating myself out of sight, but where I could both see and hear what passed, I waited for what should follow. Dr Garden and John Masey stood beside the bed. There was a moment's pause.

'I want a looking glass,' said Strange, without a word of preface.

We all started, to hear him say those words.

'I am dying,' said Strange; 'will you not grant me my request?'

Doctor Garden whispered to old Masey, and the latter left the room. He was not absent long, having gone no further than the next house. He held an oval-framed mirror in his hand when he returned. A shudder passed through the body of the sick man as he saw it.

'Put it down,' he said, faintly; 'anywhere – for the present.'

None of us spoke. I do not think, in that moment of suspense, that we *could*, any of us, have spoken if we had tried.

The sick man tried to raise himself a little. 'Prop me up,' he said. 'I speak with difficulty – I have something to say.'

They put pillows behind him, so as to raise his head and body.

'I have presently a use for it,' he said, indicating the mirror. 'I want to see –' He stopped, and seemed to change his mind. He was sparing of his words. 'I want to tell you – all about it.' Again he was silent. Then he seemed to make a great effort and spoke once more, beginning very abruptly.

'I loved my wife fondly. I loved her – her name was Lucy. She was English, but, after we were married, we lived long abroad – in Italy. She liked the country, and I liked what she liked. She liked to draw, too, and I got her a master. He was an Italian. I will not give his name. We always called him "the Master". A treacherous, insidious man this was, and, under cover of his profession, took advantage of his opportunities, and taught my wife to love him – to love him.

'I am short of breath. I need not enter into details as to how I found them out – but I *did* find them out. We were away on a sketching expedition when I made my discovery. My rage maddened me, and there was one at hand who fomented my madness. My wife had a maid, who, it seemed, had also loved this man – the Master – and had been ill-treated and deserted by him. She told me all. She had played the part of go-between – had carried letters. When she told me these things, it was night, in a solitary Italian town, among the mountains. "He is in his room now," she said, "writing to her."

'A frenzy took possession of me as I listened to those words. I am naturally vindictive – remember that – and now my longing for revenge was like a thirst. Travelling in those lonely regions, I was armed, and when the woman said, "He is writing to your wife," I laid hold of my pistols, as by an instinct. It has been some comfort to me since, that I took them both. Perhaps, at that moment, I may have meant fairly by him – meant that we should fight. I don't know what I meant, quite. The woman's words, "He is in his own room now, writing to her", rung in my ears.'

The sick man stopped to take breath. It seemed an hour, though it was probably not more than two minutes, before he spoke again.

'I managed to get into his room unobserved. Indeed, he was altogether absorbed in what he was doing. He was sitting at the only table in the room, writing at a travelling desk, by the light of a single candle. It was a rude dressing table, and – and before him – exactly before him – there was – there was a looking glass.

'I stole up behind him as he sat and wrote by the light of the candle. I looked over his shoulder at the letter, and I read, "Dearest Lucy, my love, my darling". As I read the words, I pulled the trigger of the pistol I held in my right hand and killed him – killed him – but, before he died, he looked up once – not at me, but at my image before him in the glass, and his face – such a face – has been there – ever since, and mine – my face – is gone!'

He fell back exhausted, and we all pressed forward thinking that he must be dead, he lay so still.

But he had not yet passed away. He revived under the influence of stimulants. He tried to speak, and muttered indistinctly from time to time words of which we could sometimes make no sense. We understood, however, that he had been tried by an Italian tribunal, and had been found guilty; but with such extenuating circumstances that his sentence was commuted to imprisonment, during – we thought we made out – two years. But we could not understand what he said about his wife, though we gathered that she was still alive from something he whispered to the doctor of there being provision made for her in his will.

He lay in a doze for something more than an hour after he had told his tale, and then he woke up quite suddenly, as he had done when we had first entered the room. He looked round uneasily in all directions, until his eye fell on the looking glass.

'I want it,' he said, hastily – but I noticed that he did not shudder now, as it was brought near. When old Masey approached, holding it in his hand, and crying like a child, Dr Garden came forward and stood between him and his master, taking the hand of poor Strange in his.

'Is this wise?' he asked. 'Is it good, do you think, to revive this misery of your life now, when it is so near its close? The chastisement of your crime,' he added, solemnly, 'has been a terrible one. Let us hope in God's mercy that your punishment is over.'

The dying man raised himself with a last great effort, and looked up at the doctor with such an expression on his face as none of us had seen on any face before.

'I do hope so,' he said, faintly, 'but you must let me have my way in this – for if, now, when I look, I see aright – once more – I shall then hope yet more strongly – for I shall take it as a sign.'

The doctor stood aside without another word when he heard the dying man speak thus and the old servant drew near, and, stooping over softly, held the looking glass before his master. Presently afterwards, we, who stood around looking breathlessly at him, saw such a rapture upon his face as left no doubt upon our minds that the face which had haunted him so long had, in his last hour, disappeared.

No. 4 BRANCH LINE. THE TRAVELLING POST OFFICE
[by Hesba Stretton]

Many years ago, and before this line was so much as projected, I was engaged as a clerk in a travelling post office running along the line of railway from London to a town in the Midland Counties, which we will call Fazeley. My duties were to accompany the mail train which left Fazeley at 8.15 p.m. and arrived in London about midnight, and to return by the day mail leaving London at 10.30 the following morning, after which I had an unbroken night at Fazeley, while another clerk discharged the same round of work; and in this way each alternate evening I was on duty in the railway post office van. At first I suffered a little from a hurry and tremor of nerve in pursuing my occupation while the train was crashing along under bridges and through tunnels at a speed which was then thought marvellous and perilous; but it was not long before my hands and eyes became accustomed to the motion of the carriage, and I could go through my business with the same dispatch and ease as in the post office of the country town where I had learnt it, and from which I had been promoted by the influence of the surveyor of the district, Mr Huntingdon. In fact, the work soon fell into a monotonous routine, which, night after night, was pursued in an unbroken course by myself and the junior clerk, who was my only assistant: the railway post office work not having then attained the importance and magnitude it now possesses.

Our route lay through an agricultural district containing many small towns, which made up two or three bags only: one for London, another perhaps for the county town, a third for the railway post office, to be opened by us, and the enclosures to be distributed according to their various addresses. The clerks in many of these small offices were women, as is very generally the case still, being the daughters and female relatives of the nominal postmaster, who transact most of the business of the office, and whose names are most frequently signed upon the bills accompanying the bags. I was a young man, and somewhat more curious in feminine handwriting than I am now. There was one family in particular whom I had never seen, but with whose signatures I was perfectly familiar – clear, delicate and educated, very unlike the miserable scrawl upon other letter-bills. One New Year's Eve, in a moment of sentiment, I tied a slip of paper among a bundle of letters for their office, upon which I had written, 'A happy New Year to you all'. The next evening brought me a return of my good wishes, signed, as I guessed, by three sisters of the name of Clifton. From that day, every now and then, a sentence or two as brief as the one above passed between us, and the feeling of acquaintance and friendship grew upon me, though I had never yet had an opportunity of seeing my fair unknown friends.

It was towards the close of the following October that it came under my notice that the then premier of the ministry was paying an autumn visit to a nobleman, whose country seat was situated near a small village on our line of rail. The premier's dispatch box – containing, of course, all the dispatches which it was necessary to send down to him – passed between him and the Secretary of State and was, as usual, entrusted to the care of the post office. The Continent was just then in a more than ordinarily critical state; we were thought to be upon the verge of a European war, and there were murmurs floating about, at the dispersion of the ministry up and down the country. These circumstances made the charge of the dispatch box the more interesting to me. It was very similar in size and shape to the old-fashioned workboxes used by ladies before boxes of polished and ornamental wood came into vogue, and, like them, it was covered with red morocco leather, and it fastened with a lock and key. The first time it came into my hands I took such special notice of it as might be expected. Upon one corner of the lid I detected a peculiar device scratched slightly upon it, most probably with the sharp point of a steel pen, in such a moment of preoccupation of mind as causes most of us to draw odd lines and caricatured faces upon any piece of paper which may lie under our hand. It was the old revolutionary device of a heart with a dagger piercing it, and I wondered whether it could be the premier, or one of his secretaries, who had traced it upon the morocco.

This box had been travelling up and down for about ten days and – as the village did not make up a bag for London, there being very few letters excepting those from the great house – the letter-bag from the house and the dispatch box were handed direct into our travelling post office. But in compliment to the presence of the premier in the neighbourhood, the train, instead of slackening speed only, stopped altogether, in order that the premier's trusty and confidential messenger might deliver the important box into my own hands, that its perfect safety might be ensured. I had an undefined suspicion that some person was also employed to accompany the train up to London, for three or four times I had met with a foreign-looking gentleman at Euston Square, standing at the door of the carriage nearest the post office van, and eyeing the heavy bags as they were transferred from my care to the custody of the officials from the General Post Office. But though I felt amused and somewhat nettled at this needless precaution, I took no further notice of the man, except to observe that he had the swarthy aspect of a foreigner, and that he kept his face well away from the light of the lamps. Except for these things, and after the first time or two, the premier's dispatch box interested me no more than any other part of my charge. My work had been doubly monotonous for some time past, and I began to think it time to get up some little entertainment with my unknown friends, the Cliftons. I was just thinking of it as the train stopped at the station about a mile from the town where they lived, and their postman, a gruff matter-of-fact fellow – you could see it in every line of his face – put in the letter-bags, and with them a letter addressed to me. It was in an official envelope, 'On Her Majesty's Service', and the seal was an official seal. On the folded paper inside it (folded officially also) I read the following order: 'Mr Wilcox is requested to permit the bearer, the daughter of the postmaster at Eaton, to see the working of the railway post office during the up-journey.' The writing I knew well as being that of one of the surveyor's clerks, and the signature was Mr Huntingdon's. The bearer of the order presented herself at the door, the snorting of the engine gave notice of the instant departure of the train, I held out my hand, the young lady sprang lightly and deftly into the van, and we were off again on our midnight journey.

She was a small slight creature, one of those slender little girls one never thinks of as being a woman, dressed neatly and plainly in a dark dress, with a veil hanging a little over her face and tied under her chin: the most noticeable thing about her appearance being a great mass of light hair, almost yellow, which had got loose in some way and fell down her neck in thick wavy tresses. She had a free, pleasant way about her, not in the least bold or forward, which in a minute or two made her presence seem the most natural thing in the world. As she stood beside me before the row of boxes into which I was sorting my letters, she asked questions and I answered as if it were quite an everyday occurrence for us to be travelling up together in the night mail to Euston Square station. I blamed myself for an idiot that I had not sooner made an opportunity for visiting my unknown friends at Eaton.

'Then,' I said, putting down the letter-bill from their own office before her, 'may I ask which of the signatures I know so well is yours? Is it A. Clifton, or M. Clifton, or S. Clifton?' She hesitated a little and blushed, and lifted up her frank childlike eyes to mine.

'I am A. Clifton,' she answered.

'And your name?' I said.

'Anne.' Then, as if anxious to give some explanation to me of her present position, she added, 'I was going up to London on a visit, and I thought it would be so nice to travel in the post office to see how the work was done, and Mr Huntingdon came to survey our office, and he said he would send me an order.'

I felt somewhat surprised, for a stricter martinet than Mr Huntingdon did not breathe; but I glanced down at the small innocent face at my side, and cordially approved of his departure from ordinary rules.

'Did you know you would travel with me?' I asked, in a lower voice, for Tom Morville, my junior, was at my other elbow.

'I knew I should travel with Mr Wilcox,' she answered, with a smile that made all my nerves tingle.

'You have not written me a word for ages,' said I, reproachfully.

'You had better not talk, or you'll be making mistakes,' she replied, in an arch tone. It was quite true: for, a sudden confusion coming over me, I was sorting the letters at random.

We were just then approaching the small station where the letter-bag from the great house was taken up. The engine was slackening speed. Miss Clifton manifested some natural and becoming diffidence.

'It would look so odd,' she said, 'to anyone on the platform, to see a girl in the post office van! And they couldn't know I was a postmaster's daughter, and had an order from Mr Huntingdon. Is there no dark corner to shelter me?'

I must explain to you in a word or two the construction of the van, which was much less efficiently fitted up than the travelling post offices of the present day. It was a reversible van, with a door at each right-hand corner. At each door the letter boxes were so arranged as to form a kind of screen about two feet in width, which prevented people from seeing all over the carriage at once. Thus the door at the far end of the van, the one not in use at the time, was thrown into deep shadow, and the screen before it turned it into a small niche, where a slight little person like Miss Clifton was very well concealed from curious eyes. Before the train came within the light from the lamps on the platform, she ensconced herself in this shelter. No one but I could see her laughing face, as she stood there leaning cautiously forward with her finger pressed upon her rosy lips, peeping at the messenger who delivered into my own hands the premier's dispatch box, while Tom Morville received the letter-bag of the great house.

'See,' I said, when we were again in motion, and she had emerged from her concealment, 'this is the premier's dispatch box, going back to the Secretary of State. There are some state secrets for you, and ladies are fond of secrets.'

'Oh! I know nothing about politics,' she answered, indifferently, 'and we have had that box through our office a time or two.'

'Did you ever notice this mark upon it,' I asked – 'a heart with a dagger through it?' and, bending down my face to hers, I added a certain spoony remark, which I do not care to repeat. Miss Clifton tossed her little head and pouted her lips, but she took the box out of my hands and carried it to the lamp nearest the further end of the van, after which she put it down upon the counter close beside the screen, and I thought no more about it. The midnight ride was entertaining in the extreme, for the girl was full of young life and sauciness and merry humour. I can safely aver that I have never been to an evening's so-called entertainment which, to me, was half so enjoyable. It added also to the zest and keen edge of the enjoyment to see her hasten to hide herself whenever I told her we were going to stop to take up the mails.

We had passed Watford, the last station at which we stopped, before I became alive to the recollection that our work was terribly behind-hand. Miss Clifton also became grave, and sat at the end of the counter very quiet and subdued, as if her frolic were over, and it was possible she might find something to repent of in it. I had told her we should stop no more until we reached Euston Square station, but to my surprise I felt our speed decreasing and our train coming to a standstill. I looked out and called to the guard in the van behind, who told me he supposed there was something on the line before us, and that we should go on in a minute or two. I turned my head and gave this information to my fellow clerk and Miss Clifton.

'Do you know where we are?' she asked, in a frightened tone.

'At Camden Town,' I replied. She sprang hastily from her seat and came towards me.

'I am close to my friend's house here,' she said, 'so it is a lucky thing for me. It is not five minutes' walk from the station. I will say goodbye to you now, Mr Wilcox, and I thank you a thousand times for your kindness.'

She seemed flurried, and she held out both her little hands to me in an appealing kind of way, as if she were afraid of my detaining her against her will. I took them both into mine, pressing them with rather more ardour than was quite necessary.

'I do not like you to go alone at this hour,' I said, 'but there is no help for it. It has been a delightful time to me. Will you allow me to call upon you tomorrow morning early, for I leave London at 10.30 – or on Wednesday, when I shall be in town again?'

'Oh,' she answered, hanging her head, 'I don't know. I'll write and tell mamma how kind you have been, and, and – but I must go, Mr Wilcox.'

'I don't like your going alone,' I repeated.

'Oh! I know the way perfectly,' she said, in the same flurried manner, 'perfectly, thank you. And it is close at hand. Goodbye!'

She jumped lightly out of the carriage, and the train started on again at the same instant. We were busy enough, as you may suppose. In five minutes more we should be in Euston Square, and there was nearly fifteen minutes' work still to be done. Spite of the enjoyment he had afforded me, I mentally anathematised Mr Huntingdon and his departure from ordinary rules, and, thrusting Miss Clifton forcibly out of my thoughts, I set to work with a will, gathered up the registered letters for London, tied them into bundle with the paper-bill, and then turned to the corner of the counter for the dispatch box.

You have guessed already my cursed misfortune. The premier's dispatch box was not there. For the first minute or so I was in no wise alarmed, and merely looked round – upon the floor, under the bags, into the boxes, into any place into which it could have fallen or been deposited. We reached Euston Square while I was still searching, and losing more and more of my composure every instant. Tom Morville joined me in my quest, and felt every bag which had been made up and sealed. The box was no small article which could go into little compass – it was certainly twelve inches long, and more than that in girth. But it turned up nowhere. I never felt nearer fainting than at that moment.

'Could Miss Clifton have carried it off?' suggested Tom Morville.

'No,' I said, indignantly but thoughtfully, 'she couldn't have carried off such a bulky thing as that without our seeing it. It would not go into one of our pockets, Tom, and she wore a tight-fitting jacket that would not conceal anything.'

'No, she can't have it,' assented Tom; 'then it must be somewhere about.' We searched again and again, turning over everything in the van, but without success. The premier's dispatch box was gone; and all we could do at first was to stand and stare at one another. Our trance of blank dismay was of short duration, for the van was assailed by the postmen from St Martin's-le-Grand, who were waiting for our charge. In a stupor of bewilderment we completed our work and delivered up the mails; then, once more we confronted one another with pale faces, frightened out of our seven senses. All the scrapes we had ever been in (and we had had our usual share of errors and blunders) faded into utter insignificance compared with this. My eye fell upon Mr Huntingdon's order lying among some scraps of waste paper on the floor, and I picked it up and put it carefully, with its official envelope, into my pocket.

'We can't stay here,' said Tom. The porters were looking in inquisitively; we were seldom so long in quitting our empty van.

'No,' I replied, a sudden gleam of sense darting across the blank bewilderment of my brain; 'no, we must go to headquarters at once and make a clean breast of it. This is no private business, Tom.'

We made one more ineffectual search, and then we hailed a cab and drove as hard as we could to the General Post Office. The secretary of the Post Office was not there, of course, but we obtained the address of his residence in one of the suburbs, four or five miles from the City, and we told no one of our misfortune, my idea being that the fewer who were made acquainted with the loss the better. My judgement was in the right there.

We had to knock up the household of the secretary – a formidable personage with whom I had never been brought into contact before – and in a short time we were holding a strictly private and confidential interview with him, by the glimmer of a solitary candle, just serving to light up his severe face, which changed its expression several times as I narrated the calamity. It was too stupendous for rebuke, and I fancied his eyes softened with something like commiseration as he gazed upon us. After a short interval of deliberation, he announced his intention of accompanying us to the residence of the Secretary of State, and in a few minutes we were driving back again to the opposite extremity of London. It was not far off the hour for the morning delivery of letters when we reached our destination, but the atmosphere was yellow with fog, and we could see nothing as we passed along in almost utter silence, for neither of us ventured to speak, and the secretary only made a brief remark now and then. We drove up to some dwelling enveloped in fog, and we were left in the cab for nearly half an hour, while our secretary went in. At the end of that time we were summoned to an apartment where there was seated at a large desk a small spare man, with a great head, and eyes deeply sunk under the brows. There was no form of introduction, of course, and we could only guess who he might be, but we were requested to repeat our statement, and a few shrewd questions were put to us by the stranger. We were eager to put him in possession of everything we knew, but that was little beyond the fact that the dispatch box was lost.

'That young person must have taken it,' he said.

'She could not, sir,' I answered, positively, but deferentially. 'She wore the tightest-fitting pelisse I ever saw, and she gave me both her hands when she said goodbye. She could not possibly have it concealed about her. It would not go into my pocket.'

'How did she come to travel up with you in the van, sir?' he asked, severely.

I gave him for answer the order signed by Mr Huntingdon. He and our secretary scanned it closely.

'It is Huntingdon's signature without doubt,' said the latter; 'I could swear to it anywhere. This is an extraordinary circumstance!'

It was an extraordinary circumstance. The two retired into an adjoining room, where they stayed for another half-hour, and when they returned to us their faces still bore an aspect of grave perplexity.

'Mr Wilcox and Mr Morville,' said our secretary, 'it is expedient that this affair should be kept inviolably secret. You must even be careful not to hint that you hold any secret. You did well not to announce your loss at the Post Office, and I shall cause it to be understood that you had instructions to take the dispatch box direct to its destination. Your business now is to find the young woman, and return with her not later than six o'clock this afternoon to my office at the General Post Office. What other steps we think it requisite to take, you need know nothing about – the less you know, the better for yourselves.'

Another gleam of commiseration in his official eye made our hearts sink within us. We departed promptly and, with that instinct of wisdom which at times dictates infallibly what course we should pursue, we decided our line of action. Tom Morville was to go down to Camden Town and enquire at every house for Miss Clifton, while I – there would be just time for it – was to run down to Eaton by train and obtain her exact address from her parents. We agreed to meet at the General Post Office at half-past five, if I could possibly reach it by that time; but in any case Tom was to report himself to the secretary, and account for my absence.

When I arrived at the station at Eaton, I found that I had only forty-five minutes before the up-train went by. The town was nearly a mile away, but I made all the haste I could to reach it. I was not surprised to find the post office in connection with a bookseller's shop, and I saw a pleasant elderly lady seated behind the counter, while a tall dark-haired girl was sitting at some work a little out of sight. I introduced myself at once.

'I am Frank Wilcox, of the railway post office, and I have just run down to Eaton to obtain some information from you.'

'Certainly. We know you well by name,' was the reply, given in a cordial manner, which was particularly pleasant to me.

'Will you be so good as give me the address of Miss Anne Clifton in Camden Town?' I said.

'Miss Anne Clifton?' ejaculated the lady.

'Yes. Your daughter, I presume. Who went up to London last night.'

'I have no daughter Anne,' she said; 'I am Anne Clifton, and my daughters are named Mary and Susan. This is my daughter Mary.'

The tall dark-haired girl had left her seat and now stood beside her mother. Certainly she was very unlike the small golden-haired coquette who had travelled up to London with me as Anne Clifton.

'Madam,' I said, scarcely able to speak, 'is your other daughter a slender little creature, exactly the reverse of this young lady?'

'No,' she answered, laughing; 'Susan is both taller and darker than Mary. Call Susan, my dear.'

In a few seconds Miss Susan made her appearance, and I had the three before me – A. Clifton, S. Clifton, and M. Clifton. There was no other girl in the family; and when I described the young lady who had travelled under their name, they could not think of anyone in the town – it was a small one – who answered my description, or who had gone on a visit to London. I had no time to spare, and I hurried back to the station, just catching the train as it left the platform. At the appointed hour I met Morville at the General Post Office and, threading the long passages of the secretary's offices, we at length found ourselves anxiously waiting in an ante-room, until we were called into his presence. Morville had discovered nothing, except that the porters and policemen at Camden Town station had seen a young lady pass out last night, attended by a swarthy man who looked like a foreigner, and carried a small black portmanteau.

I scarcely know how long we waited; it might have been years, for I was conscious of an ever-increasing difficulty in commanding my thoughts, or fixing them upon the subject which had engrossed them all day. I had not tasted food for twenty-four hours, nor closed my eyes for thirty-six, while, during the whole of the time, my nervous system had been on full strain.

Presently the summons came, and I was ushered, first, into the inner apartment. There sat five gentlemen round a table, which was strewn with a number of documents. There were the Secretary of State, whom we had seen in the morning, our secretary and Mr Huntingdon; the fourth was a fine-looking man, whom I afterwards knew to be the premier; the fifth I recognised as our great chief, the postmaster general. It was an august assemblage to me, and I bowed low, but my head was dizzy, and my throat parched.

'Mr Wilcox,' said our secretary, 'you will tell these gentlemen again the circumstances of the loss you reported to me this morning.'

I laid my hand upon the back of a chair to steady myself, and went through the narration for the third time, passing over sundry remarks made by myself to the young lady. That done, I added the account of my expedition to Eaton, and the certainty at which I had arrived that my fellow-traveller was not the person she represented herself to be. After which, I enquired with indescribable anxiety if Mr Huntingdon's order were a forgery?

'I cannot tell, Mr Wilcox,' said that gentleman, taking the order into his hands, and regarding it with an air of extreme perplexity. 'I could have sworn it was mine, had it been attached to any other document. I think Forbes's handwriting is not so well imitated. But it is the very ink I use, and mine is a peculiar signature.'

It was a very peculiar and old-fashioned signature, with a flourish underneath it not unlike a whip handle, with the lash caught round it in the middle; but that did not make it the more difficult to forge, as I humbly suggested. Mr Huntingdon wrote his name upon a paper, and two or three of the gentlemen tried to imitate the flourish, but vainly. They gave it up with a smile upon their grave faces.

'You have been careful not to let a hint of this matter drop from you, Mr Wilcox?' said the postmaster general.

'Not a syllable, my lord,' I answered.

'It is imperatively necessary that the secret should be kept. You would be removed from the temptation of telling it, if you had an appointment in some office abroad. The packet agency at Alexandria is vacant, and I will have you appointed to it at once.'

It would be a good advance from my present situation, and would doubtless prove a stepping stone to other and better appointments; but I had a mother living at Fazeley, bedridden and paralytic, who had no pleasure in existence except having me to dwell under the same roof with her. My head was growing more and more dizzy, and a strange vagueness was creeping over me.

'Gentlemen,' I muttered, 'I have a bedridden mother whom I cannot leave. I was not to blame, gentlemen.' I fancied there was a stir and movement at the table, but my eyes were dim, and in another second I had lost consciousness.

When I came to myself, in two or three minutes, I found that Mr Huntingdon was kneeling on the floor beside me, supporting my head, while our secretary held a glass of wine to my lips. I rallied as quickly as possible, and staggered to my feet; but the two gentlemen placed me in the chair against which I had been leaning, and insisted upon my finishing the wine before I tried to speak.

'I have not tasted food all day,' I said, faintly.

'Then, my good fellow, you shall go home immediately,' said the postmaster general; 'but be on your guard! Not a word of this must escape you. Are you a married man?'

'No, my lord,' I answered.

'So much the better,' he added, smiling. 'You can keep a secret from your mother, I dare say. We rely upon your honour.'

The secretary then rang a bell, and I was committed to the charge of the messenger who answered it; and in a few minutes I was being conveyed in a cab to my London lodgings. A week afterwards, Tom Morville was sent out to a post office in Canada, where he settled down, married, and is still living, perfectly satisfied with his position, as he occasionally informs me by letter. For myself, I remained as I desired, in my old post as travelling clerk until the death of my mother, which occurred some ten or twelve months afterwards. I was then promoted to an appointment as a clerk in charge, upon the first vacancy.

The business of the clerks in charge is to take possession of any post office in the kingdom, upon the death or resignation of the postmaster, or when circumstances of suspicion cause his suspension from office. My new duties carried me three or four times into Mr Huntingdon's district. Though that gentleman and I never exchanged a word with regard to the mysterious loss in which we had both had an innocent share, he distinguished me with peculiar favour, and more than once invited me to visit him at his own house. He lived alone, having but one daughter, who had married, somewhat against his will, one of his clerks: the Mr Forbes whose handwriting had been so successfully imitated in the official order presented to me by the self-styled Miss Anne Clifton. (By the way, I may here mention, though it has nothing to do with my story, that my acquaintance with the Cliftons had ripened into an intimacy, which resulted in my engagement and marriage to Mary.)

It would be beside my purpose to specify the precise number of years which elapsed before I was once again summoned to the secretary's private apartment, where I found him closeted with Mr Huntingdon. Mr Huntingdon shook hands with unofficial cordiality, and then the secretary proceeded to state the business on hand.

'Mr Wilcox, you remember our offer to place you in office in Alexandria?' he said.

'Certainly, sir,' I answered.

'It has been a troublesome office,' he continued, almost pettishly. 'We sent out Mr Forbes only six months ago, on account of his health, which required a warmer climate, and now his medical man reports that his life is not worth three weeks' purchase.'

Upon Mr Huntingdon's face there rested an expression of profound anxiety; and as the secretary paused he addressed himself to me.

'Mr Wilcox,' he said, 'I have been soliciting, as a personal favour, that you should be sent out to take charge of the packet agency, in order that my daughter may have someone at hand to befriend her, and manage her business affairs for her. You are not personally acquainted with her, but I know I can trust her with you.'

'You may, Mr Huntingdon,' I said, warmly. 'I will do anything I can to aid Mrs Forbes. When do you wish me to start?'

'How soon can you be ready?' was the rejoinder.

'Tomorrow morning.'

I was not married then, and I anticipated no delay in setting off. Nor was there any. I travelled with the overland mail through France to Marseilles, embarked in a vessel for Alexandria, and in a few days from the time I first heard of my destination, set foot in the office there. All the postal arrangements had fallen into considerable irregularity and confusion; for, as I was informed immediately on my arrival, Mr Forbes had been in a dying condition for the last week, and of course the absence of a master had borne the usual results. I took formal possession of the office, and then, conducted by one of the clerks, I proceeded to the dwelling of the unfortunate postmaster and his no less unfortunate wife. It would be out of place in this narrative to indulge in any traveller's tales about the strange place where I was so unexpectedly located. Suffice it to say that the darkened sultry room into which I was shown, on enquiring for Mrs Forbes, was bare of furniture, and destitute of all those little tokens of refinement and taste which make our English parlours so pleasant to the eye. There was, however, a piano in one of the dark corners of the room, open and with a sheet of music on it. While I waited for Mrs Forbes's appearance, I strolled idly up to the piano to see what music it might be. The next moment my eye fell upon an antique red morocco workbox standing on the top of the piano – a workbox evidently, for the lid was not closely shut, and a few threads of silk and cotton were hanging out of it. In a kind of dream – for it was difficult to believe that the occurrence was a fact – I carried the box to the darkened window, and there, plain in my sight, was the device scratched upon the leather: the revolutionary symbol of a heart with a dagger through it. I had found the premier's dispatch box in the parlour of the packet agent of Alexandria!

I stood for some minutes with that dreamlike feeling upon me, gazing at the box in the dim obscure light. It could *not* be real! My fancy must be playing a trick upon me! But the sound of a light step – for, light as it was, I heard it distinctly as it approached the room – broke my trance, and I hastened to replace the box on the piano, and to stoop down as if examining the music before the door opened. I had not sent in my name to Mrs Forbes, for I did not suppose that she was acquainted with it, nor could she see me distinctly, as I stood in the gloom. But I could see her. She had the slight slender figure, the childlike face and the fair hair of Miss Anne Clifton. She came quickly across the room, holding out both her hands in a childish appealing manner.

'Oh!' she wailed, in a tone that went straight to my heart, 'he is dead! He has just died!'

It was no time then to speak about the red morocco workbox. This little childish creature, who did not look a day older than when I had last seen her in my travelling post office, was a widow in a strange land, far away from any friend save myself. I had brought her a letter from her father. The first duties that devolved upon me were those of her husband's interment, which had to take place immediately. Three or four weeks elapsed before I could, with any humanity, enter upon the investigation of her mysterious complicity in the daring theft practised on the government and the post office.

I did not see the dispatch box again. In the midst of her new and vehement grief, Mrs Forbes had the precaution to remove it before I was ushered again into the room where I had discovered it. I was at some trouble to hit upon any plan by which to gain a second sight of it; but I was resolved that Mrs Forbes should not leave Alexandria without giving me a full explanation. We were waiting for remittances and instructions from England, and in the meantime the violence of her grief abated, and she recovered a good share of her old buoyancy and loveliness, which had so delighted me on my first acquaintance with her. As her demands upon my sympathy weakened, my curiosity grew stronger, and at last mastered me. I carried with me a netted purse which required mending, and I asked her to catch up the broken meshes while I waited for it.

'I will tell your maid to bring your workbox,' I said, going to the door and calling the servant. 'Your mistress has a red morocco workbox,' I said to her, as she answered my summons.

'Yes, sir,' she replied.

'Where is it?'

'In her bedroom,' she said.

'Mrs Forbes wishes it brought here.' I turned back into the room. Mrs Forbes had gone deadly pale, but her eyes looked sullen, and her teeth were clenched under her lips with an expression of stubbornness. The maid brought the workbox. I walked, with it in my hands, up to the sofa where she was seated.

'You remember this mark?' I asked; 'I think neither of us can ever forget it.'

She did not answer by word, but there was a very intelligent gleam in her blue eyes.

'Now,' I continued, softly, 'I promised your father to befriend you, and I am not a man to forget a promise. But you must tell me the whole simple truth.'

I was compelled to reason with her, and to urge her for some time. I confess I went so far as to remind her that there was an English consul at Alexandria, to whom I could resort. At last she opened her stubborn lips, and the whole story came out, mingled with sobs and showers of tears.

She had been in love with Alfred, she said, and they were too poor to marry, and papa would not hear of such a thing. She was always in want of money, she was kept so short; and they promised to give her such a great sum – a vast sum – five hundred pounds.

'But who bribed you?' I enquired.

A foreign gentleman whom she had met in London, called Monsieur Bonnard. It was a French name, but she was not sure that he was a Frenchman. He talked to her about her father being a surveyor in the post office, and asked her a great number of questions. A few weeks after, she met him in their own town by accident, she and Mr Forbes; and Alfred had a long private talk with him, and they came to her, and told her she could help them very much. They asked her if she could be brave enough to carry off a little red box out of the travelling post office, containing nothing but papers. After a while she consented. When she had confessed so much under compulsion, Mrs Forbes seemed to take a pleasure in the narrative, and went on fluently.

'We required papa's signature to the order, and we did not know how to get it. Luckily he had a fit of the gout and was very peevish; and I had to read over a lot of official papers to him, and then he signed them. One of the papers I read twice, and slipped the order into its place after the second reading. I thought I should have died with fright, but just then he was in great pain, and glad to get his work over. I made an excuse that I was going to visit my aunt at Beckby, but instead of going there direct, we contrived to be at the station at Eaton a minute or two before the mail train came up. I kept outside the station door till we heard the whistle, and just then the postman came running down the road, and I followed him straight through the booking office, and asked him to give you the order, which I put into his hand. He scarcely saw me. I just caught a glimpse of Monsieur Bonnard's face through the window of the compartment next to the van, when Alfred had gone. They had promised me that the train should stop at Camden Town, if I could only keep your attention engaged until then. You know how I succeeded.'

'But how did you dispose of the box?' I asked. 'You could not have concealed it about you – that I am sure of.'

'Ah!' she said, 'nothing was easier. Monsieur Bonnard had described the van to me, and you remember I put the box down at the end of the counter, close to the corner where I hid myself at every station. There was a door with a window in it, and I asked if I might have the window open, as the van was too warm for me. I believe Monsieur Bonnard could have taken it from me by only leaning through his window, but he preferred stepping out, and taking it from my hand, just as the train was leaving Watford – on the far side of the carriages, you understand. It was the last station, and the train came to a stand at Camden Town. After all, the box was not out of your sight more than twenty minutes before you missed it. Monsieur Bonnard and I hurried out of the station, and Alfred followed us. The box was forced open – the lock has never been mended, for it was a peculiar one – and Monsieur Bonnard took possession of the papers. He left the box with me, after putting inside it a roll of notes. Alfred and I were married next morning, and I went back to my aunt's; but we did not tell papa of our marriage for three or four months. That is the story of my red morocco workbox.'

She smiled with the provoking mirthfulness of a mischievous child. There was one point still, on which my curiosity was unsatisfied.

'Did you know what the dispatches were about?' I asked.

'Oh no!' she answered; 'I never understood politics in the least. I knew nothing about them. Monsieur did not say a word; he did not even look at the papers while we were by. I would never, never, have taken a registered letter or anything with money in it, you know. But all those papers could be written again quite easily. You must not think me a thief, Mr Wilcox; there was nothing worth money among the papers.'

'They were worth five hundred pounds to you,' I said. 'Did you ever see Bonnard again?'

'Never again,' she replied. 'He said he was going to return to his native country. I don't think Bonnard was his real name.'

Most likely not, I thought; but I said no more to Mrs Forbes. Once again I was involved in a great perplexity about this affair. It was clearly my duty to report the discovery at headquarters, but I shrank from doing so. One of the chief culprits was already gone to another judgement than that of man; several years had obliterated all traces of Monsieur Bonnard; and the only victim of justice would be this poor little dupe of the two greater criminals. At last I came to the conclusion to send the whole of the particulars to Mr Huntingdon himself; and I wrote them to him, without remark or comment.

The answer that came to Mrs Forbes and me in Alexandria was the announcement of Mr Huntingdon's sudden death of some disease of the heart, on the day which I calculated would put him in possession of my communication. Mrs Forbes was again over-whelmed with apparently heart-rending sorrow and remorse. The income left to her was something less than one hundred pounds a year. The secretary of the post office, who had been a personal friend of the deceased gentleman, was his sole executor; and I received a letter from him, containing one for Mrs Forbes, which recommended her, in terms not to be misunderstood, to fix upon some residence abroad, and not to return to England. She fancied she would like the seclusion and quiet of a convent; and I made arrangements for her to enter one in Malta, where she would still be under British protection. I left Alexandria myself on the arrival of another packet agent, and on my return to London I had a private interview with the secretary. I found that there was no need to inform him of the circumstances I have related to you, as he had taken possession of all Mr Huntingdon's papers. In consideration of his ancient friendship, and of the escape of those who most merited punishment, he had come to the conclusion that it was quite as well to let bygones be bygones.

At the conclusion of the interview I delivered a message which Mrs Forbes had emphatically entrusted to me.

'Mrs Forbes wished me to impress upon your mind,' I said, 'that neither she nor Mr Forbes would have been guilty of this misdemeanour if they had not been very much in love with one another, and very much in want of money.'

'Ah!' replied the secretary, with a smile, 'if Cleopatra's nose had been shorter, the fate of the world would have been different!'

No. 5 BRANCH LINE. THE ENGINEER
[by Amelia Edwards]

His name, sir, was Matthew Price; mine is Benjamin Hardy. We were born within a few days of each other, bred up in the same village, taught at the same school. I cannot remember the time when we were not close friends. Even as boys, we never knew what it was to quarrel. We had not a thought, we had not a possession that was not in common. We would have stood by each other, fearlessly, to the death. It was such a friendship as one reads about sometimes in books: fast and firm as the great tors upon our native moorlands, true as the sun in the heavens.

The name of our village was Chadleigh. Lifted high above the pasture flats which stretched away at our feet like a measureless green lake and melted into mist on the furthest horizon, it nestled, a tiny stone-built hamlet, in a sheltered hollow about midway between the plain and the plateau. Above us, rising ridge beyond ridge, slope beyond slope, spread the mountainous moor country, bare and bleak for the most part, with here and there a patch of cultivated field or hardy plantation, and crowned highest of all with masses of huge grey crag, abrupt, isolated, hoary, and older than the deluge. These were the tors – druid's tor, king's tor, castle tor, and the like – sacred places, as I have heard, in the ancient time, where crownings, burnings, human sacrifices and all kinds of bloody heathen rites were performed. Bones, too, had been found there, and arrowheads, and ornaments of gold and glass. I had a vague awe of the tors in those boyish days, and would not have gone near them after dark for the heaviest bribe.

I have said that we were born in the same village. He was the son of a small farmer, named William Price, and the eldest of a family of seven; I was the only child of Ephraim Hardy, the Chadleigh blacksmith – a well-known man in those parts, whose memory is not forgotten to this day. Just so far as a farmer is supposed to be a bigger man than a blacksmith, Mat's father might be said to have a better standing than mine; but William Price with his small holding and his seven boys was, in fact, as poor as many a day-labourer; whilst the blacksmith, well-to-do, bustling, popular and open-handed, was a person of some importance in the place. All this, however, had nothing to do with Mat and myself. It never occurred to either of us that his jacket was out at elbows, or that our mutual funds came altogether from my pocket. It was enough for us that we sat on the same school bench, conned our tasks from the same primer, fought each other's battles, screened each other's faults, fished, nutted, played truant, robbed orchards and birds' nests together, and spent every half-hour, authorised or stolen, in each other's society. It was a happy time – but it could not go on for ever. My father, being prosperous, resolved to put me forward in the world. I must know more, and do better, than himself. The forge was not good enough, the little world of Chadleigh was not wide enough, for me. Thus it happened that I was still swinging the satchel when Mat was whistling at the plough, and that at last, when my future course was shaped out, we were separated, as it then seemed to us, for life. For, blacksmith's son as I was, furnace and forge, in some form or other, pleased me best, and I chose to be a working engineer. So my father by and by apprenticed me to a Birmingham ironmaster; and, having bidden farewell to Mat and Chadleigh, and the grey old tors in the shadow of which I had spent all the days of my life, I turned my face northward, and went over into 'the Black Country'.

I am not going to dwell on this part of my story. How I worked out the term of my apprenticeship; how, when I had served my full time and become a skilled workman, I took Mat from the plough and brought him over to the Black Country, sharing with him lodging, wages, experience (all, in short, that I had to give); how he, naturally quick to learn and brimful of quiet energy, worked his way up a step at a time and came by and by to be a 'first hand' in his own department; how, during all these years of change and trial and effort, the old boyish affection never wavered or weakened, but went on, growing with our growth and strengthening with our strength – are facts which I need do no more than outline in this place.

About this time – it will be remembered that I speak of the days when Mat and I were on the bright side of thirty – it happened that our firm contracted to supply six first-class locomotives to run on the new line, then in process of construction, between Turin and Genoa. It was the first Italian order we had taken. We had had dealings with France, Holland, Belgium, Germany, but never with Italy. The connection, therefore, was new and valuable – all the more valuable because our transalpine neighbours had but lately begun to lay down the iron roads, and would be safe to need more of our good English work as they went on. So the Birmingham firm set themselves to the contract with a will, lengthened our working hours, increased our wages, took on fresh hands, and determined, if energy and promptitude could do it, to place themselves at the head of the Italian labour market and stay there. They deserved and achieved success. The six locomotives were not only turned out to time, but were shipped, dispatched and delivered with a promptitude that fairly amazed our Piedmontese consignee. I was not a little proud, you may be sure, when I found myself appointed to superintend the transport of the engines. Being allowed a couple of assistants, I contrived that Mat should be one of them; and thus we enjoyed together the first great holiday of our lives.

It was a wonderful change for two Birmingham operatives fresh from the Black Country. The fairy city, with its crescent background of Alps; the port crowded with strange shipping; the marvellous blue sky and bluer sea; the painted houses on the quays; the quaint cathedral, faced with black and white marble; the street of jewellers, like an Arabian Nights' bazaar; the street of palaces, with its Moorish courtyards, its fountains and orange trees; the women veiled like brides; the galley slaves chained two and two; the processions of priests and friars; the everlasting clangour of bells; the babble of a strange tongue; the singular lightness and brightness of the climate – made, altogether, such a combination of wonders that we wandered about, the first day, in a kind of bewildered dream, like children at a fair. Before that week was ended, being tempted by the beauty of the place and the liberality of the pay, we had agreed to take service with the Turin and Genoa Railway Company, and to turn our backs upon Birmingham for ever.

Then began a new life – a life so active and healthy, so steeped in fresh air and sunshine, that we sometimes marvelled how we could have endured the gloom of the Black Country. We were constantly up and down the line: now at Genoa, now at Turin, taking trial trips with the locomotives, and placing our old experiences at the service of our new employers.

In the meanwhile we made Genoa our headquarters, and hired a couple of rooms over a small shop in a by-street sloping down to the quays. Such a busy little street – so steep and winding that no vehicles could pass through it, and so narrow that the sky looked like a mere strip of deep-blue ribbon overhead! Every house in it, however, was a shop, where the goods encroached on the footway, or were piled about the door, or hung like tapestry from the balconies; and all day long, from dawn to dusk, an incessant stream of passers-by poured up and down between the port and the upper quarter of the city.

Our landlady was the widow of a silver-worker, and lived by the sale of filigree ornaments, cheap jewellery, combs, fans and toys in ivory and jet. She had an only daughter named Giannetta, who served in the shop, and was simply the most beautiful woman I ever beheld. Looking back across this weary chasm of years, and bringing her image before me (as I can and do) with all the vividness of life, I am unable, even now, to detect a flaw in her beauty. I do not attempt to describe her. I do not believe there is a poet living who could find the words to do it; but I once saw a picture that was somewhat like her (not half so lovely, but still like her), and, for aught I know, that picture is still hanging where I last looked at it – upon the walls of the Louvre. It represented a woman with brown eyes and golden hair, looking over her shoulder into a circular mirror held by a bearded man in the background. In this man, as I then understood, the artist had painted his own portrait; in her, the portrait of the woman he loved.[5] No picture that I ever saw was half so beautiful, and yet it was not worthy to be named in the same breath with Giannetta Coneglia.

You may be certain the widow's shop did not want for customers. All Genoa knew how fair a face was to be seen behind that dingy little counter; and Giannetta, flirt as she was, had more lovers than she cared to remember, even by name. Gentle and simple, rich and poor, from the red-capped sailor buying his earrings or his amulet, to the nobleman carelessly purchasing half the filigrees in the window, she treated them all alike – encouraged them, laughed at them, led them on and turned them off at her pleasure. She had no more heart than a marble statue – as Mat and I discovered by and by, to our bitter cost.

I cannot tell to this day how it came about, or what first led me to suspect how things were going with us both; but long before the waning of that autumn a coldness had sprung up between my friend and myself. It was nothing that could have been put into words. It was nothing that either of us could have explained or justified to save his life. We lodged together, ate together, worked together, exactly as before – we even took our long evening's walk together, when the day's labour was ended – and except, perhaps, that we were more silent than of old, no mere looker-on could have detected a shadow of change. Yet there it was, silent and subtle, widening the gulf between us every day.

It was not his fault. He was too true and gentle-hearted to have willingly brought about such a state of things between us. Neither do I believe – fiery as my nature is – that it was mine. It was all hers – hers from first to last – the sin, and the shame, and the sorrow.

If she had shown a fair and open preference for either of us, no real harm could have come of it. I would have put any constraint upon myself, and – Heaven knows! – have borne any suffering, to see Mat really happy. I know that he would have done the same, and more if he could, for me. But Giannetta cared not one sou for either. She never meant to choose between us. It gratified her vanity to divide us; it amused her to play with us. It would pass my power to tell how, by a thousand imperceptible shades of coquetry – by the lingering of a glance, the substitution of a word, the flitting of a smile – she contrived to turn our heads and torture our hearts, and lead us on to love her. She deceived us both. She buoyed us both up with hope; she maddened us with jealousy; she crushed us with despair. For my part, when I seemed to wake to a sudden sense of the ruin that was about our path and I saw how the truest friendship that ever bound two lives together was drifting on to wreck and ruin, I asked myself whether any woman in the world was worth what Mat had been to me and I to him. But this was not often. I was readier to shut my eyes upon the truth than to face it; and so lived on, wilfully, in a dream.

Thus the autumn passed away, and winter came – the strange, treacherous Genoese winter, green with olive and ilex, brilliant with sunshine, and bitter with storm. Still, rivals at heart and friends on the surface, Mat and I lingered on in our lodging in the Vicolo Balba. Still Giannetta held us with her fatal wiles and her still more fatal beauty. At length there came a day when I felt I could bear the horrible misery and suspense of it no longer. The sun, I vowed, should not go down before I knew my sentence. She must choose between us. She must either take me or let me go. I was reckless. I was desperate. I was determined to know the worst, or the best. If the worst, I would at once turn my back upon Genoa, upon her, upon all the pursuits and purposes of my past life, and begin the world anew. This I told her, passionately and sternly, standing before her in the little parlour at the back of the shop, one bleak December morning.

'If it's Mat whom you care for most,' I said, 'tell me so in one word, and I will never trouble you again. He is better worth your love. I am jealous and exacting; he is as trusting and unselfish as a woman. Speak, Giannetta; am I to bid you goodbye for ever and ever, or am I to write home to my mother in England, bidding her pray to God to bless the woman who has promised to be my wife?'

'You plead your friend's cause well,' she replied, haughtily. 'Matteo ought to be grateful. This is more than he ever did for you.'

'Give me my answer, for pity's sake,' I exclaimed, 'and let me go!'

'You are free to go or stay, Signor Inglese,' she replied. 'I am not your jailer.'

'Do you bid me leave you?'

'*Beata Madre*![6] Not I.'

'Will you marry me, if I stay?'

She laughed aloud – such a merry, mocking, musical laugh, like a chime of silver bells!

'You ask too much,' she said.

'Only what you have led me to hope these five or six months past!'

'That is just what Matteo says. How tiresome you both are!'

'O, Giannetta,' I said, passionately, 'be serious for one moment! I am a rough fellow, it is true – not half good enough or clever enough for you – but I love you with my whole heart, and an emperor could do no more.'

'I am glad of it,' she replied; 'I do not want you to love me less.'

'Then you cannot wish to make me wretched! Will you promise me?'

'I promise nothing,' said she, with another burst of laughter; 'except that I will not marry Matteo!'

Except that she would not marry Matteo! Only that. Not a word of hope for myself. Nothing but my friend's condemnation. I might get comfort, and selfish triumph, and some sort of base assurance out of that, if I could. And so, to my shame, I did. I grasped at the vain encouragement, and – fool that I was! – let her put me off again unanswered. From that day, I gave up all effort at self-control, and let myself drift blindly on – to destruction.

At length things became so bad between Mat and myself that it seemed as if an open rupture must be at hand. We avoided each other, scarcely exchanged a dozen sentences in a day, and fell away from all our old familiar habits. At this time – I shudder to remember it! – there were moments when I felt that I hated him.

Thus, with the trouble deepening and widening between us day by day, another month or five weeks went by, and February came – and, with February, the Carnival. They said in Genoa that it was a particularly dull carnival – and so it must have been, for, save a flag or two hung out in some of the principal streets, and a sort of *festa*[7] look about the women, there were no special indications of the season. It was, I think, the second day when, having been on the line all the morning, I returned to Genoa at dusk and, to my surprise, found Mat Price on the platform. He came up to me, and laid his hand on my arm.

'You are in late,' he said. 'I have been waiting for you three quarters of an hour. Shall we dine together today?'

Impulsive as I am, this evidence of returning good will at once called up my better feelings.

'With all my heart, Mat,' I replied; 'shall we go to Gozzoli's?'

'No, no,' he said, hurriedly. 'Some quieter place – some place where we can talk. I have something to say to you.'

I noticed now that he looked pale and agitated, and an uneasy sense of apprehension stole upon me. We decided on the 'Pescatore', a little out-of-the-way trattoria, down near the Molo Vecchio. There, in a dingy salon, frequented chiefly by seamen, and redolent of tobacco, we ordered our simple dinner. Mat scarcely swallowed a morsel; but, calling presently for a bottle of Sicilian wine, drank eagerly.

'Well, Mat,' I said, as the last dish was placed on the table, 'what news have you?'

'Bad.'

'I guessed that from your face.'

'Bad for you – bad for me. Giannetta.'

'What of Giannetta?'

He passed his hand nervously across his lips.

'Giannetta is false – worse than false,' he said, in a hoarse voice. 'She values an honest man's heart just as she values a flower for her hair – wears it for a day, then throws it aside for ever. She has cruelly wronged us both.'

'In what way? Good Heavens, speak out!'

'In the worst way that a woman can wrong those who love her. She has sold herself to the Marchese Loredano.'

The blood rushed to my head and face in a burning torrent. I could scarcely see, and dared not trust myself to speak.

'I saw her going towards the cathedral,' he went on, hurriedly. 'It was about three hours ago. I thought she might be going to confession, so I hung back and followed her at a distance. When she got inside, however, she went straight to the back of the pulpit, where this man was waiting for her. You remember him – an old man who used to haunt the shop a month or two back. Well, seeing how deep in conversation they were, and how they stood close under the pulpit with their backs towards the church, I fell into a passion of anger and went straight up the aisle, intending to say or do something: I scarcely knew what; but, at all events, to draw her arm through mine and take her home. When I came within a few feet, however, and found only a big pillar between myself and them, I paused. They could not see me, nor I them; but I could hear their voices distinctly, and – and I listened.'

'Well, and you heard –'

'The terms of a shameful bargain – beauty on the one side, gold on the other; so many thousand francs a year; a villa near Naples – Pah! It makes me sick to repeat it.'

And, with a shudder, he poured out another glass of wine and drank it at a draught.

'After that,' he said, presently, 'I made no effort to bring her away. The whole thing was so cold-blooded, so deliberate, so shameful, that I felt I had only to wipe her out of my memory and leave her to her fate. I stole out of the cathedral and walked about here by the sea for ever so long, trying to get my thoughts straight. Then I remembered you, Ben; and the recollection of how this wanton had come between us and broken up our lives drove me wild. So I went up to the station and waited for you. I felt you ought to know it all; and – and I thought, perhaps, that we might go back to England together.'

'The Marchese Loredano!'

It was all that I could say – all that I could think. As Mat had just said of himself, I felt 'like one stunned'.

'There is one other thing I may as well tell you,' he added, reluctantly, 'if only to show you how false a woman can be. We – we were to have been married next month.'

'*We*? Who? What do you mean?'

'I mean that we were to have been married – Giannetta and I.'

A sudden storm of rage, of scorn, of incredulity, swept over me at this, and seemed to carry my senses away.

'*You!*' I cried. 'Giannetta marry you! I don't believe it.'

'I wish I had not believed it,' he replied, looking up as if puzzled by my vehemence. 'But she promised me – and I thought, when she promised it, she meant it.'

'She told me, weeks ago, that she would never be your wife!'

His colour rose, his brow darkened; but when his answer came, it was as calm as the last.

'Indeed!' he said. 'Then it is only one baseness more. She told me that she had refused you, and that was why we kept our engagement secret.'

'Tell the truth, Mat Price,' I said, well-nigh beside myself with suspicion. 'Confess that every word of this is false! Confess that Giannetta will not listen to you, and that you are afraid I may succeed where you have failed. As perhaps I shall – as perhaps I shall, after all!'

'Are you mad?' he exclaimed. 'What do you mean?'

'That I believe it's just a trick to get me away to England – that I don't credit a syllable of your story. You're a liar, and I hate you!'

He rose and, laying one hand on the back of his chair, looked me sternly in the face.

'If you were not Benjamin Hardy,' he said, deliberately, 'I would thrash you within an inch of your life.'

The words had no sooner passed his lips than I sprang at him. I have never been able distinctly to remember what followed. A curse – a blow – a struggle – a moment of blind fury – a cry – a confusion of tongues – a circle of strange faces. Then I see Mat lying back in the arms of a by-stander – myself trembling and bewildered – the knife dropping from my grasp – blood upon the floor – blood upon my hands – blood upon his shirt. And then I hear those dreadful words:

'O, Ben, you have murdered me!'

He did not die – at least, not there and then. He was carried to the nearest hospital, and lay for some weeks between life and death. His case, they said, was difficult and dangerous. The knife had gone in just below the collarbone, and pierced down into the lungs. He was not allowed to speak or turn – scarcely to breathe with freedom. He might not even lift his head to drink. I sat by him day and night all through that sorrowful time. I gave up my situation on the railway; I quitted my lodging in the Vicolo Balba; I tried to forget that such a woman as Giannetta Coneglia had ever drawn breath. I lived only for Mat, and he tried to live more, I believe, for my sake than his own. Thus, in the bitter silent hours of pain and penitence, when no hand but mine approached his lips or smoothed his pillow, the old friendship came back with even more than its old trust and faithfulness. He forgave me, fully and freely – and I would thankfully have given my life for him.

At length there came one bright spring morning, when, dismissed as convalescent, he tottered out through the hospital gates, leaning on my arm, and feeble as an infant. He was not cured – neither, as I then learnt to my horror and anguish, was it possible that he ever could be cured. He might live, with care, for some years; but the lungs were injured beyond hope of remedy, and a strong or healthy man he could never be again. These, spoken aside to me, were the parting words of the chief physician, who advised me to take him further south without delay.

I took him to a little coast town called Rocca, some thirty miles beyond Genoa – a sheltered lonely place along the Riviera, where the sea was even bluer than the sky, and the cliffs were green with strange tropical plants, cacti, and aloes, and Egyptian palms. Here we lodged in the house of a small tradesman – and Mat, to use his own words, 'set to work at getting well in good earnest'. But, alas! It was a work which no earnestness could forward. Day after day he went down to the beach, and sat for hours drinking the sea air and watching the sails that came and went in the offing. By and by he could go no further than the garden of the house in which we lived. A little later, and he spent his days on a couch beside the open window, waiting patiently for the end. Ay, for the end! It had come to that. He was fading fast, waning with the waning summer, and conscious that the Reaper was at hand. His whole aim now was to soften the agony of my remorse, and prepare me for what must shortly come.

'I would not live longer, if I could,' he said, lying on his couch one summer evening, and looking up to the stars. 'If I had my choice at this moment, I would ask to go. I should like Giannetta to know that I forgave her.'

'She shall know it,' I said, trembling suddenly from head to foot.

He pressed my hand.

'And you'll write to father?'

'I will.'

I had drawn a little back, that he might not see the tears raining down my cheeks; but he raised himself on his elbow and looked round.

'Don't fret, Ben,' he whispered, laid his head back wearily upon the pillow – and so died.

And this was the end of it. This was the end of all that made life life to me. I buried him there, in hearing of the wash of a strange sea on a strange shore. I stayed by the grave till the priest and the bystanders were gone. I saw the earth filled in to the last sod, and the gravedigger stamp it down with his feet. Then, and not till then, I felt that I had lost him for ever – the friend I had loved, and hated, and slain. Then, and not till then, I knew that all rest and joy and hope were over for me. From that moment my heart hardened within me, and my life was filled with loathing. Day and night, land and sea, labour and rest, food and sleep, were alike hateful to me. It was the curse of Cain, and that my brother had pardoned me made it lie none the lighter. Peace on earth was for me no more, and goodwill towards men was dead in my heart for ever. Remorse softens some natures, but it poisoned mine. I hated all mankind, but above all mankind I hated the woman who had come between us two, and ruined both our lives.

He had bidden me seek her out, and be the messenger of his forgiveness. I had sooner have gone down to the port of Genoa and taken upon me the serge cap and shotted chain of any galley-slave at his toil in the public works; but for all that I did my best to obey him. I went back, alone and on foot. I went back, intending to say to her, 'Giannetta Coneglia, he forgave you – but God never will.' But she was gone. The little shop was let to a fresh occupant, and the neighbours only knew that mother and daughter had left the place quite suddenly, and that Giannetta was supposed to be under the 'protection' of the Marchese Loredano. How I made enquiries here and there – how I heard that they had gone to Naples – and how, being restless and reckless of my time, I worked my passage in a French steamer and followed her – how, having found the sumptuous villa that was now hers, I learnt that she had left there some ten days and gone to Paris, where the Marchese was ambassador for the Two Sicilies[8] – how, working my passage back again to Marseilles, and thence, in part by the river and in part by the rail, I made my way to Paris – how, day by day, I paced the streets and the parks, watched at the ambassador's gates, followed his carriage, and at last, after weeks of waiting, discovered her address – how, having written to request an interview, her servants spurned me from her door and flung my letter in my face – how, looking up at her windows, I then, instead of forgiving, solemnly cursed her with the bitterest curses my tongue could devise – and how, this done, I shook the dust of Paris from my feet and became a wanderer upon the face of the earth – are facts which I have now no space to tell.

The next six or eight years of my life were shifting and unsettled enough. A morose and restless man, I took employment here and there, as opportunity offered, turning my hand to many things, and caring little what I earned, so long as the work was hard and the change incessant. First of all I engaged myself as chief engineer in one of the French steamers plying between Marseilles and Constantinople. At Constantinople I changed to one of the Austrian Lloyd's boats, and worked for some time to and from Alexandria, Jaffa, and those parts. After that, I fell in with a party of Mr Layard's men at Cairo, and so went up the Nile and took a turn at the excavations of the mound of Nimroud.[9] Then I became a working engineer on the new desert line between Alexandria and Suez; and by and by I worked my passage out to Bombay and took service as an engine fitter on one of the great Indian railways. I stayed a long time in India – that is to say, I stayed nearly two years, which was a long time for me – and I might not even have left so soon, but for the war that was declared just then with Russia. That tempted me. For I loved danger and hardship as other men love safety and ease; and as for my life, I had sooner have parted from it than kept it, any day. So I came straight back to England; betook myself to Portsmouth, where my testimonials at once procured me the sort of berth I wanted. I went out to the Crimea in the engine room of one of Her Majesty's war steamers.

I served with the fleet, of course, while the war lasted; and when it was over, went wandering off again, rejoicing in my liberty. This time I went to Canada, and after working on a railway then in progress near the American frontier, I presently passed over into the States; journeyed from north to south; crossed the Rocky Mountains; tried a month or two of life in the Gold Country; and then, being seized with a sudden, aching, unaccountable longing to revisit that solitary grave so far away on the Italian coast, I turned my face once more towards Europe.

Poor little grave! I found it rank with weeds, the cross half shattered, the inscription half effaced. It was as if no one had loved him, or remembered him. I went back to the house in which we had lodged together. The same people were still living there, and made me kindly welcome. I stayed with them for some weeks. I weeded, and planted, and trimmed the grave with my own hands, and set up a fresh cross in pure white marble. It was the first season of rest that I had known since I laid him there; and when at last I shouldered my knapsack and set forth again to battle with the world, I promised myself that, God willing, I would creep back to Rocca, when my days drew near to ending, and be buried by his side.

From hence, being perhaps a little less inclined than formerly for very distant parts, and willing to keep within reach of that grave, I went no further than Mantua, where I engaged myself as an engine-driver on the line, then not long completed, between that city and Venice. Somehow, although I had been trained to the working engineering, I preferred in these days to earn my bread by driving. I liked the excitement of it, the sense of power, the rush of the air, the roar of the fire, the flitting of the landscape. Above all, I enjoyed to drive a night express. The worse the weather, the better it suited with my sullen temper. For I was as hard, and harder than ever. The years had done nothing to soften me. They had only confirmed all that was blackest and bitterest in my heart.

I continued pretty faithful to the Mantua line, and had been working on it steadily for more than seven months when that which I am now about to relate took place.

It was in the month of March. The weather had been unsettled for some days past, and the nights stormy; and at one point along the line, near Ponte di Brenta, the waters had risen and swept away some seventy yards of embankment. Since this accident, the trains had all been obliged to stop at a certain spot between Padua and Ponte di Brenta, and the passengers, with their luggage, had thence to be transported in all kinds of vehicles, by a circuitous country road, to the nearest station on the other side of the gap, where another train and engine awaited them. This, of course, caused great confusion and annoyance, put all our timetables wrong, and subjected the public to a large amount of inconvenience. In the meanwhile an army of navvies was drafted to the spot, and worked day and night to repair the damage. At this time I was driving two through-trains each day – namely, one from Mantua to Venice in the early morning, and a return train from Venice to Mantua in the afternoon – a tolerably full day's work, covering about one hundred and ninety miles of ground, and occupying between ten and eleven hours. I was therefore not best pleased when, on the third or fourth day after the accident, I was informed that, in addition to my regular allowance of work, I should that evening be required to drive a special train to Venice. This special train, consisting of an engine, a single carriage and a break-van, was to leave the Mantua platform at eleven; at Padua the passengers were to alight and find post-chaises waiting to convey them to Ponte di Brenta; at Ponte di Brenta another engine, carriage and break-van were to be in readiness. I was charged to accompany them throughout.

'*Corpo di Bacco*,' said the clerk who gave me my orders, 'you need not look so black, man. You are certain of a handsome gratuity. Do you know who goes with you?'

'Not I.'

'Not you, indeed! Why, it's the Duca Loredano, the Neapolitan ambassador.'

'Loredano!' I stammered. 'What Loredano? There was a Marchese –'

'*Certo*. He was the Marchese Loredano some years ago, but he has come into his dukedom since then.'

'He must be a very old man by this time.'

'Yes, he is old; but what of that? He is as hale and bright and stately as ever. You have seen him before?'

'Yes,' I said, turning away; 'I have seen him – years ago.'

'You have heard of his marriage?'

I shook my head.

The clerk chuckled, rubbed his hands and shrugged his shoulders.

'An extraordinary affair,' he said. 'Made a tremendous esclandre[10] at the time. He married his mistress – quite a common, vulgar girl – a Genoese – very handsome, but not received, of course. Nobody visits her.'

'Married her!' I exclaimed. 'Impossible.'

'True, I assure you.'

I put my hand to my head. I felt as if I had had a fall or a blow.

'Does she – does she go tonight?' I faltered.

'Oh dear, yes – goes everywhere with him – never lets him out of her sight. You'll see her – *la bella Duchessa!*'

With this my informant laughed and rubbed his hands again, and went back to his office.

The day went by, I scarcely know how, except that my whole soul was in a tumult of rage and bitterness. I returned from my afternoon's work about 7.25, and at 10.30 I was once again at the station. I had examined the engine; given instructions to the *fochista*, or stoker, about the fire; seen to the supply of oil; and got all in readiness when, just as I was about to compare my watch with the clock in the ticket office, a hand was laid upon my arm, and a voice in my ear said:

'Are you the engine-driver who is going on with this special train?'

I had never seen the speaker before. He was a small, dark man, muffled up about the throat, with blue glasses, a large black beard and his hat drawn low upon his eyes.

'You are a poor man, I suppose,' he said, in a quick, eager whisper, 'and, like other poor men, would not object to be better off. Would you like to earn a couple of thousand florins?'

'In what way?'

'Hush! You are to stop at Padua, are you not, and to go on again at Ponte di Brenta?'

I nodded.

'Suppose you did nothing of the kind. Suppose, instead of turning off the steam, you jump off the engine and let the train run on?'

'Impossible. There are seventy yards of embankment gone, and –'

'*Basta!*[11] I know that. Save yourself, and let the train run on. It would be nothing but an accident.'

I turned hot and cold – I trembled – my heart beat fast and my breath failed.

'Why do you tempt me?' I faltered.

'For Italy's sake,' he whispered; 'for liberty's sake. I know you are no Italian; but, for all that, you may be a friend. This Loredano is one of his country's bitterest enemies. Stay, here are the two thousand florins.'

I thrust his hand back fiercely.

'No – no,' I said. 'No blood money. If I do it, I do it neither for Italy nor for money, but for vengeance.'

'For vengeance!' he repeated.

At this moment the signal was given for backing up to the platform. I sprang to my place upon the engine without another word. When I again looked towards the spot where he had been standing, the stranger was gone.

I saw them take their places – Duke and Duchess, secretary and priest, valet and maid. I saw the stationmaster bow them into the carriage and stand, bareheaded, beside the door. I could not distinguish their faces – the platform was too dusky, and the glare from the engine fire too strong – but I recognised her stately figure and the poise of her head. Had I not been told who she was, I should have known her by those traits alone. Then the guard's whistle shrilled out, and the station-master made his last bow. I turned the steam on, and we started.

My blood was on fire. I no longer trembled or hesitated. I felt as if every nerve was iron, and every pulse instinct with deadly purpose. She was in my power, and I would be revenged. She should die – she, for whom I had stained my soul with my friend's blood! She would die, in the plenitude of her wealth and her beauty, and no power upon earth should save her!

The stations flew past. I put on more steam – I bade the fireman heap in the coke and stir the blazing mass. I would have outstripped the wind, had it been possible. Faster and faster – hedges and trees, bridges and stations, flashing past – villages no sooner seen than gone – telegraph wires twisting and dipping and twining themselves in one, with the awful swiftness of our pace! Faster and faster, till the fireman at my side looks white and scared, and refuses to add more fuel to the furnace. Faster and faster, till the wind rushes in our faces and drives the breath back upon our lips.

I would have scorned to save myself. I meant to die with the rest. Mad as I was – and I believe from my very soul that I was utterly mad for the time – I felt a passing pang of pity for the old man and his suite. I would have spared the poor fellow at my side too, if I could; but the pace at which we were going made escape impossible.

Vicenza was passed – a mere confused vision of lights. Pojana flew by. At Padua, but nine miles distant, our passengers were to alight. I saw the fireman's face turned upon me in remonstrance; I saw his lips move, though I could not hear a word; I saw his expression change suddenly from remonstrance to a deadly terror, and then – merciful Heaven! – then, for the first time, I saw that he and I were no longer alone upon the engine.

There was a third man – a third man standing on my right hand, as the fireman was standing on my left – a tall, stalwart man, with short curling hair and a flat Scotch cap upon his head. As I fell back in the first shock of surprise, he stepped nearer; took my place at the engine, and turned the steam off. I opened my lips to speak to him; he turned his head slowly, and looked me in the face.

Matthew Price!

I uttered one long wild cry, flung my arms wildly up above my head, and fell as if I had been smitten with an axe.

I am prepared for the objections that may be made to my story. I expect, as a matter of course, to be told that this was an optical illusion, or that

I was suffering from pressure on the brain, or even that I laboured under an attack of temporary insanity. I have heard all these arguments before and, if I may be forgiven for saying so, I have no desire to hear them again. My own mind has been made up upon this subject for many a year. All that I can say – all that I *know* is – that Matthew Price came back from the dead to save my soul and the lives of those whom I, in my guilty rage, would have hurried to destruction. I believe this as I believe in the mercy of Heaven and the forgiveness of repentant sinners.

NOTES

1. Eternal.

2. A malapropism for 'basilisk'.

3. The Great Exhibition was an international exhibition held in London from May to October 1851. It was the first in a series of exhibitions of culture and industry that were to be a popular feature of nineteenth century life.

4. Working men's secret orders which brought financial relief to those afflicted by illness through a common fund.

5. Probably a reference to Titian's (*c.*1488–1576) painting *Woman with a Mirror* (*c.*1513–5).

6. 'Blessed Mother', i.e. the Virgin Mary (Italian).

7. Literally 'festival' – used attributatively, as it is here, it could be translated as 'festive' (Italian).

8. In 1816, Naples and Sicily were amalgamated to form the Kingdom of the Two Sicilies.

9. In the mid-nineteenth century, Sir Austen Henry Layard (1817–1894) excavated the mounds of Nimroud, the site of the biblical city Calah.

10. An event which gives rise to scandal. The term is taken directly from French.

11. 'Enough' (Italian).

BIOGRAPHICAL NOTES

Charles Dickens (1812-70) was one of Victorian England's most popular and prolific authors. A journalist and editor, he was also instrumental in identifying and encouraging some of his most significant writing contemporaries. Dickens' early life was financially and emotionally unstable, and when his father was imprisoned for debt, he was sent to work in a blacking factory, an experience which haunted his later fiction. Dickens worked as an office boy and court reporter before his *Sketches by Boz* (1836-37) brought his writing to the attention of the publishing house Chapman and Hall. After the success of *The Posthumous Papers of the Pickwick Club*, Dickens was able to found the journal *Bentley's Miscellany*, and from then on all his major novels were published as serial instalments in his own magazines. Dickens remained a tireless social reformer and popular public figure all his life. He died suddenly, leaving his novel, *The Mystery of Edwin Drood*, unfinished.

Andrew Halliday (1830-77) was a writer, journalist and dramatist. He contributed many articles to Dickens' *All the Year Round* magazine and numerous other publications. He also wrote and co-wrote many successful plays and theatrical adaptations, including *Little Em'ly* (1869), a very popular adaptation of David Copperfield.

Charles Collins (1828-73) was a painter and writer – and the brother of Wilkie Collins. He was a close friend of Millais and associated himself in his youth with the Pre-Raphaelite Brotherhood. His most famous painting from that period was the 1851 'Convent Thoughts'. He married Dickens' daughter Kate in 1860, although her father did not entirely approve of this union, partly because of his financial difficulties and ill health. In order to ease his son-in-law's situation, Dickens employed him on *All the Year Round* and commissioned illustrations from him for the *The Mystery of Edwin Drood*. He died of stomach cancer in 1873.

Hesba Stretton (a.k.a. Sarah Smith, 1832-1911) was the author of popular religious books for children, including *Jessica's First Prayer*, which sold over one and a half million copies. Stretton, who was a friend of Dickens' and a regular contributor to his journals, also co-founded the N.S.P.C.C.

Amelia Edwards (1831–92) was a novelist, journalist and Egyptologist, who wrote prolifically and precociously – her first poem was published at the age of 7; her first story at the age of 12. She enjoyed considerable success with her articles, stories and novels – including *Barbara's History* (1864) and *Lord Brackenbury* (1880) – but she became even more famous for her travel writing and her interest in the archaeology of Ancient Egypt, founding the Egypt Exploration Fund with Reginald Poole and working tirelessly to gain support and recognition for this cause. She is also remembered for her active involvement in the suffragettes' movement.

SELECTED TITLES FROM HESPERUS PRESS

Author	Title	Foreword writer
Jane Austen	*Love and Friendship*	Fay Weldon
Aphra Behn	*The Lover's Watch*	
Charlotte Brontë	*The Green Dwarf*	Libby Purves
Emily Brontë	*Poems of Solitude*	Helen Dunmore
Anton Chekhov	*Three Years*	William Fiennes
Wilkie Collins	*Who Killed Zebedee?*	Martin Jarvis
William Congreve	*Incognita*	Peter Ackroyd
Joseph Conrad	*The Return*	Colm Tóibín
Charles Dickens	*The Haunted House*	Peter Ackroyd
Fyodor Dostoevsky	*The Double*	Jeremy Dyson
George Eliot	*Amos Barton*	Matthew Sweet
Henry Fielding	*Jonathan Wild the Great*	Peter Ackroyd
F. Scott Fitzgerald	*The Rich Boy*	John Updike
E.M. Forster	*Arctic Summer*	Anita Desai
Elizabeth Gaskell	*Lois the Witch*	Jenny Uglow
Thomas Hardy	*Fellow-Townsmen*	Emma Tennant
L.P. Hartley	*Simonetta Perkins*	Margaret Drabble
Nathaniel Hawthorne	*Rappaccini's Daughter*	Simon Schama
John Keats	*Fugitive Poems*	Andrew Motion
D.H. Lawrence	*Daughters of the Vicar*	Anita Desai
Katherine Mansfield	*In a German Pension*	Linda Grant
Prosper Mérimée	*Carmen*	Philip Pullman
Sándor Petőfi	*John the Valiant*	George Szirtes
Alexander Pope	*The Rape of the Lock*	Peter Ackroyd
Robert Louis Stevenson	*Dr Jekyll and Mr Hyde*	Helen Dunmore
Leo Tolstoy	*Hadji Murat*	Colm Tóibín
Mark Twain	*Tom Sawyer, Detective*	
Oscar Wilde	*The Portrait of Mr W.H.*	Peter Ackroyd
Virginia Woolf	*Carlyle's House and Other Sketches*	Doris Lessing